One
Bone
Rattle

David Putnam

IAMPRESS
Memphis, TN

Danny!
Thanks for
a great meal
& Ambiance

7-21-05

One Bone Rattle

David Putnam

Original Cover Art

Jennifer Ragan

First Edition
Copyright © 2004

Although this book is based loosely on some true events in the life of someone personal to the author, it is primarily fiction. Any similarity to actual persons, places, or events is not intended by the author or publisher. Such similarities are purely coincidental and are rendered forth in this text without liability.

IAMPress

Memphis, TN

Copyright © 2004
by David Putnam

Printed in the United States of America
ISBN 1-59196-762-7

Dedication

*To my dad, Dick…who always encouraged me
to do what some thought me incapable of doing,
and in the doing, solidify the faith in me
others had all the while.*

Preface

It was a bright sunny day in Nashville on April 16, 1984. The dogwood trees were in full bloom and the buttercups and jonquils seem to add to the brightness of the sun's rays. Dick had gone to get the day's mail from the box. The trip to and from the box wore him out. The chemotherapy had taken its toll on the 62 year old.

Finally, he made it to the patio and sat down in a lawn chair underneath the umbrella that blossomed out of the table like a giant flower. He laid the mail on top of the wire mesh table. At first, he sat gasping to get air into his lungs, then softer gulps, then normal breathing. It seemed like hours to Dick, but in actual time, just a few minutes went by.

He began to thumb through the pile of ads and bills when his fingers caressed an envelope of a texture he didn't recognize. He slowly pulled it from its hiding place. His eyes scanned the front left corner of the letter and he saw the return address, C. Stringfellow/ Beauray, Louisiana.

The postmark on the stamp showed a date of April 16,1927. A smile crossed Dick's face. His hands trembled as he put a thumbnail under the edge of the sealed portion of the envelope and he sliced open the letter. He removed the old crisp sheet of folded paper and with his hands still shaking slightly, he unfolded the missive and began to read.

i

April 16, 1984

Dear Dick,

My old friend, it has been too many years since you and I talked.

I know we should have talked more, but you and I both know it would have been all the worse for you.

Now the time has come that there is no need for me to fear for your safety. The evil that existed in our youth and that has grown ever so much stronger over the years cannot harm you any more.

Your day of peace draws near. I cannot say that I will be happy that you will not be in this plain, but I can assure you that in the next existence you will be reunited with all whom you love now, and all those you have loved in the past.

My promise to you made on that day when you left us in Beauray, so many years ago, will be kept. I have set the stage for your son to hear what you and I know of men and evil and how the two are intertwined.

I will be his guide in telling him of your yesterdays and his protector when I tell him about the tenuous path that your life took.

We will talk again. I will be with you and you will hear my voice when the pain is too strong, and you will be at peace.

Your faithful friend,
Ce

Dick's head fell to his chest and he breathed a great sigh. To anyone who might have heard it, it was a sigh of relief. It mixed with a slight breeze that was blowing. In Louisiana, a man turned to feel a slight breeze upon his face, closed his eyes and said to himself, "Soon old hoss, soon." Dick died one month to the day after reading the letter.

After the funeral, Dick's wife gave her stepson David, a shoebox his father had wanted him to have. In it she told him, were letters of things his father wanted him to know about. Things she couldn't really speak about. After a tearful good-bye with his stepmother, David and his wife, Janet, headed back to Memphis.

Upon hitting the interstate, David asked Janet to open the box and read some of the letters his father had left to him out loud to pass the time on the drive. Janet said she would and opened the box by removing the lid. She looked inside and all she saw were ashes and a few crumble pieces of paper. She moved the paper around with her finger and on one small piece she could make out the word, *Ce.*

David asked her what was taking her so long? She replied that there was nothing in the box but ashes. David swerved to the emergency lane and stopped the car. He took the box from Janet's hand, looked inside for himself. The look on David's face was one of total disbelief. "What the hell is this?" he blurted out. Janet just looked at him and shrugged her shoulders. This meant to David, that she didn't have a clue as to what it meant. They set there in silence for a moment and then David said, "Shit", started the car and maneuvered back onto the interstate. Janet reached for the box top and turned it over to see who had made the shoes. On the inside of the lid was written a note. Janet recognized it as Dick's handwriting. She excitedly told David about the discovery and asked him if he wanted to hear it. He said, "please." Janet began to read the note with out ceremony.

Son, I'm sorry all you have from me is this box of ashes. I wanted to tell you things I never had time to, but now, you'll have to hear them from and old friend. *He* will, make himself known to you in his own way. Now turn on I-40 and take these ashes to my grave and poor them on top. Janet, **make him listen**!

Remember, I love you both,
Dad

iv

The I-40 exit sign loomed ahead. It took about 30 minutes to get to the cemetery from where they were. David pulled onto I-40 and drove in silence. They entered the gate leading to the new grave his father now occupied. David stopped the car and Janet and he got out and stood by the grave. Janet gave him the box containing the ashes. She held the top in her arms as if she were cradling a small child. David did as his father's note had directed him to do and poured the ashes onto the fresh earth that covered him. He stood there with Janet for a few minutes. Shaking off the morbid feelings this had brought to them, they got back into their car and continued on to Memphis. Passing through the gate again, David looked back through his rearview mirror and saw an eery shadow pass over his father's grave. The shadow seemed to be unnaturally dark and had human features. David shook his head to clear the nonsense from his mind. He looked at Janet for a second, then drove on.

Chapter One

February came and it was time for Mardi-Gras. The Santa Anna winds from California had rendered the weather in February unusually milder than normal in the southeast. I had checked the forecast for the festive stay in New Orleans and the weather was perfect for traveling as well as for the Mardi Gras.

My wife, Janet, and I had been waiting three years for this trip. Taking care to plan well in advance, we made a pact to use the time off as lovers leaving behind jobs, mundane house and yard work, and the day in, day out stresses that bog down the natural flow of romance. I had initially resisted the time-share idea when Janet suggested it years ago, but as much as we wanted to go and do, I agreed to the investment and it had become a handy little item in our travels.

Because of the way time-shares work, trying to trade your share for another can be a long process. We knew that any time around the celebration would be hard to book, so we traded our time-share two years ago for one week this particular year in New Orleans for the Mardi Gras. We had put our heads together and formed a game plan to follow in realizing this vacation.

Our son, Robert, who was living in Monroe Louisiana at that time, hinted that he would like to come over and *visit* us while we were in New Orleans. He and his girl-friend wanted to meet us at the condo on Fat Tuesday. Robert's idea of visiting with us would have entailed meeting some friends and going off to party with them. As a back up, he would have the condo with us for showers and sleep.

I tried to tell him when he suggested the visit that the whole idea behind this vacation was to allow his mother and I to have a "second honeymoon." From the tone of his voice on the phone, I guessed that was more information than he wanted to hear. However, he held to the belief that we would still let him come. Janet and I knew they would pop in and out as the mood struck them. The concept of him barging in on us at an inappropriate time ran through my mind. He and his friends could be "scarred" for life. We didn't really want to budge on the issue, but he outlasted me on the pause between spoken words and we finally said he was welcome to come.

As luck would have it though, he called us Sunday night and said he couldn't make it. His boss wanted him to put some extra time in at work to get things in shape for an inspection. If all went right, he could get a promotion out of the deal. With the news that he and the assorted folks weren't going to be around at weird times, Janet and I held to our "second honeymoon" game plan.

From Memphis, where we live, it only takes about five hours to drive straight south to New Orleans. We left early the next morning, planning to arrive in the city early enough to get a little rest at the condo, then hit the streets to immerse ourselves in the revelry and romantic atmosphere of New Orleans.

On the way to Louisiana from Tennessee down through Mississippi, it was an uneventful trip. Janet and I have never talked a lot on long driving trips. She likes to catch up on her reading and I like to keep a lookout for the possible or impossible road hazards that plague the highways, mainly other drivers.

There was one thing that did seem out of place as I was keeping an eye out along the road. As we crossed into Louisiana, I caught sight of a man walking along the side of the highway. Just an old country boy heading to town, I thought to myself. *Except* from a distance, it seemed like he had long, black hair with a white streak running down the middle. That would be unusual no matter where a person saw that kind of hair on a man. It was like an animal's.

I don't know why this struck me so odd at the time, but it was one of those thoughts that hang around and haunt a person. I tried to get Janet to look at him, but by the time she pulled away from reading the section of the book she was into, she only caught a glimpse of him in the side mirror. She asked me what she'd missed about the guy. All I could think to say was that he looked *funny*.

The condo we selected in New Orleans was situated on St. Peter Street in part of the Veux Carre area. Located on the riverfront, it was sequestered behind an old storefront that was a disguise for a roomy and modern set of suites. After arriving at the resident manager's office, we were given a quick tour by one of the staff and were surprised upon entering that the rooms of the condo were painted in a rich crimson with snow white trim around the doors and windows. The ornate cornice board around the ceiling and the egg and dart moldings used for chair railing accented the opulence of this abode. There was a full kitchen and a marble bath, thick pile carpet that made you feel like going barefoot, and a four poster bed in the master bedroom that came with a stool to get up to the mattress. We hadn't gotten any brochures to look at when we booked our trip. Usually we get an arm full, but this time we went blind and hopeful. After our tour guide left, Janet and I hugged each other; we kissed and knew this "second honeymoon" was going to be righteous!

After sitting in a car for five hours and only two stops to refresh ourselves, we were pretty antsy to get out on the town. We went and changed into the clothes that we thought more suited for the night's events. I changed my shirt from an old tank top I wore driving, to a flowered Hawaiian number; and Janet put on a slinky silk looking, dark blue dress; one with a slit up one side. We were in such a hurry to get to the streets, we left our luggage scattered around the rooms with clothes draped on chairs.

Taking to the streets, we heard the vendors hawking their beverages. Having no control over myself when it comes to drinking, I didn't see any reason to get anything but a soft drink. Alcohol has a very dramatic and sometimes dangerous effect on me. After a few drinks, I cease to be the fun loving guy that I am normally and turn into a mean drunk.

Janet sampled the drinks she liked though; Pink Panty Pull Downs, Sea Breezes, and the world famous Hurricane, which is the beverage that New Orleans is noted for. We strolled to the music and the cacophony of sounds that blared at us. Then, we danced to the rhythmic South American influences and boogied down to the American strains. After a few hours of this, the parades began we found ourselves famished. We ate at the Two Sisters restaurant that evening. I figured as long as we were going to experience the culture we should experience it as though we were in haut monde.

The Food! The food was as sumptuous as I had ever imagined. I ordered as much as I thought two people could eat. The wine list was excellent; it was arranged to accent the Cajon flavored mix of taste delights. I ordered a bottle for Janet. Our waiter was attentive and helpful with the selections, to make sure we didn't burn our non-Cajon stomachs out. I think that a lot of people come to New Orleans for the decadence, to find a fast food place, and then get so drunk that they can't see straight. Our waiter picked up on the fact that we didn't fit the social norm.

Something about our waiter though caught my eye. I'm funny about things like that. It's one of those "deja vu", physic friend things, that comes and goes. He seemed young, but then again, in the light of the white accent lights strung in the trees and the candled tables of the garden we were dining in, as he moved about he seemed to waver, or to shift from young to old and back again. I caught myself thinking I'd had sipped too much of Janet's wine at the initial tasting. I shook my head to try and clear it. Janet asked me if something was wrong, I shook myself again and said, No, not really, I just had one of those feelings, the ones you get when people say some one has stepped on your grave. I shook it off and dinner went on.

After eating we walked the streets until about 3 a.m., enjoying the sights and sounds of all that New Orleans had to offer. We walked back to the condo, two well-fed and happy people. Back at the condo the long day and evening caught up with us and we settled in for the night. We lay in that big bed and cuddled. I started to tell Janet how much I really was glad we were on this trip when I heard her breathing deepen. Along with the drinks she'd had, the long day finally took its toll and she was asleep. I reached over to the lamp on the night stand and switched off the light. After getting into our favorite spooning position I closed my eyes and within a few seconds I was out for the count.

That old saying, "Time goes by fast when you're having fun." Yeah, right. 6 a.m. found some not too happy people being awakened by some not so funny people right outside our window with a jackhammer.

I jumped up out of the bed. Poor Janet thought we were having an earthquake. After I gained some sense of where I was, I went to the window and peered down to see city workers banging away. I went into a tirade. "What the fuck are those ass wipes, cock sucking, mother fuckers, doing this shit now for?" I said as loud as I could. Janet held her hands over her ears. She looked at me and shouted for me to please make them stop.

I grabbed the phone and called the condo manager, but the line was busy. I thought that someone else was going off on him too. I could have saved the call and thrown all my anger out the window and possibly made those sons of bitches shut the hell up. When I finally got through to the manager, he said that he couldn't do any thing it was the city maintenance department. Needless to say Janet and I were not happy campers that morning.

We drug ourselves one at a time to the shower. Of course, ladies first. I went into the kitchen to set up the coffee pot. I found some Cafe du Monde coffee in the cabinet. I put the water in the tank and the coffee in the filter. I flipped the switch and the smell of fresh coffee made me feel as though I was only a pair of old socks hung out to dry, instead of the soiled sheet I was a few minutes ago.

After I showered and between shouts trying to out sound the "hammer" we headed out to the French Market to get more of the CDM coffee and beignets. We drink CDM at home but the authentic beignets can only be found in that part of the south. A beignet is a hot, sugared, and sweet tasting confectionary. When baked by a true southerner it has been known to make a man slap his momma if she tried to take it away from him. I was planning to gain 10 pounds that morning so I ordered a dozen just for myself and a paltry four for my wife.

After the caffeine and sugar rush of breakfast, Janet and I spent the morning walking around the shopping areas. We enjoyed the street performers and took a horse drawn tour around the "safe" areas located on the tourist maps. We had set up tours of the grave sights where the famous and infamous persons of New Orleans now reside, in a couple of days when the party was down to a memory and the dourness of lent had taken hold of the city we'd have things to do. Around 11:30 a.m., we headed toward the St. Louis Square. There were people setting up to do portraits, sell voodoo trinkets, and tell fortunes. Local commerce didn't stop for lent it seemed.

We noticed one vendor in particular because; well,

because he was white. Not just someone with normal white skin, but *white* skin, you know, like the old saying about *white on rice*. I guess some people would say he was almost an albino. We probably wouldn't have paid that much attention to him but his oddity stood out among all the other vendors. Where they seemed to almost jamb into each other, this person commanded his own space. Along with his whiteness he had coal black shoulder length long hair with a streak of white running down the center. I laughed to Janet that he looked like he had a skunk on his head. His black slacks, white shirt, and black vest accented his skunkiness. Then I shuddered. Janet took my right elbow in her hand and asked me if I were okay. I told her that I felt like I did at supper last night, but this time they didn't just step on my grave they did a boogie woogie, and wasn't that our waiter? No, this man was definitely too old I saw the image of the old country boy I saw on the highway when we crossed over the state lines, the one Janet didn't see.

We watched awhile as he set up his table a big umbrella and two chairs. He had placed a small sign on the edge of the table that read, "Fortunes, good or bad, $2.00 cards, or $4.00 palm".

You know how you watch a person or thing from a certain vantage point and you really don't see one particular "thing"? I mean, I never noticed his eyes until he put on a pair of sunglasses and by then I really couldn't see them. He sat down, adjusted himself for comfort, crossed his legs and folded his hands and set them in his lap. We watched him a little longer and he just sat there.

Janet asked if we could get our fortunes told. I hesitated looking around to make sure I didn't see anybody we knew and finally said okay. I don't like this kind of crap. My mother was a dabbler in this stuff and it can become obsessive with her. We walked over to "skunk head's" table and Janet sat down. In a hollow monotone voice he spoke up and said, "Cards or palm?" Thinking a moment she responded with, cards. He slowly moved to face the table and took a deck of tarot cards from a box he had under the chair. He shuffled them seven times and then he laid them out in a pattern like a diamond, one top center, one left, one right, repeating this until he had a six card diamond then he placed one in the center to make seven total. During this whole exercise he never looked up. I tried to see his eyes but his shades were like those safety glasses that have the side panels, there was just no way. He told Janet that she would be prosperous, have good health, and a long life blah, blah, blah. Janet asked him if he could be more specific about our trip to New Orleans. He told her not to worry that we would have plenty to do. He picked up the seven cards, returned them to the deck and that was that.

I was reaching in my pocket to get the $2.00 when he looked up at me and said, "sit". Janet got up from the seat looking at me. I don't know why but I sat down without question. He took my right hand.

His hands had a texture that made my skin crawl. It felt almost as though it was embalmed and his fingers were long and thin; for lack of better terms, womanish. I instinctively tried to recoil from him but he held fast. He traced my lifeline and the whole of my palm. As abruptly as he had picked up my hand, he dropped it. This next part I'll never forget. He said she was through. That's all. Nothing else. Like nothing to see here, move along. Period. Nada. Zip. I sat stunned for a moment and then I said, "What's up with this," he didn't respond. Again I said, "What's up"? All he did was sit there with his hand out for the money. Janet tapped me on the shoulder and I turned to face her, she had one of her "let's bug out now" looks. I gave her my raised eyebrow hand waving "wait a minute" looks. Then, I turned back to "skunk head" again to get some sort of answer.

When I did, he took off his shades. Man! I'm telling you, his eyes were solid black and they were deeply recessed into his face. I backed up on the chair and Janet was holding her purse like she'd been taught in one of her self-defense classes, ready to slap the piss out of this guy if he made any weird moves. He looked at both of us for a moment and then he broke into a high-pitched laugh. In between gulps of air and giggles, he said that he had contacts on his eyes. His eyes were light sensitive and these were a new set of contacts he was breaking in and the shades helped his eyes cope with the light.

He motioned for me to sit down again. His quick jovial mood just as quickly turned somber. "You really want to know? Do you really want to know?" I'd heard this voice before, somewhere, sometime, many years ago. Without thinking I nodded my head yes. He sighed deeply, almost as though he were relieved.

He looked me in the eyes and said, "All folks got skeletons, and we put them in closets the old folks say. If you open that closet, they'll all be in there, the first one of you to the last one that died. When the winds of life act up and blow, shaking all those skeletons, you'll only hear one bone rattle."

I didn't understand any of that and just shook my head again. Janet asked him what it meant. He looked at her and then at me again. He almost sobbed and muttered under his breath "it begins." He sat there a moment with his head bowed then took a long deep breath. He raised his head and looked our way again. He told us to come to a bar called Hurricanes, he would be there around midnight, and then he would elaborate.

He held out his hand again for the money so I gave a $10 and told him to keep the change. We turned to walk away and heard him say once again, "Midnight."

Chapter Two

The rest of the day was very pleasant as far as the sightseeing went. We strolled along famous Bourbon Street, Layette Street, and the rest of the "touristy" side streets. We shopped at the Dansk store on the way for a gift to give our priest's new baby, then went in and out of so many T- shirt shops I gave up on who had what. Then, we ate Po-boy's and Pralines along with sampling some gat'or tail. I am always watching for danger when Janet and I are out and especially after the incident we experienced earlier that morning. Except for the occasional freak we saw, like the vampire wannabe's all decked out in their *Gothic* attire, women who were men, men who were women, *trannies* (I think they're referred to) and the everyday scammers; nothing I saw or felt in particular raised the cockles on the back of my neck.

As the day progressed, the humidity rose with every footstep we took, drenching us in our own sweat. We almost called a cab, but decided to walk back to the condo. I don't know when the street crew quit working, but they were gone when we returned. We went straight to our rooms. Upon entering, we dropped our packages by the door, gave each other a quick smooch, then I went and spread out on the deeply padded sofa in the wonderful air-conditioned comfort of the spacious living room. Being soaked to the skin from the humidity was not even a passing thought. Within a few seconds of hitting the sofa, *I was out like a light.*

After a power nap I didn't even remember, I woke and jumped straight up off the couch. Janet had lain down on the day bed and was still fast asleep. I looked at my watch; it was almost 9 p.m. I went over to Janet, shook her shoulder and gently told her it was time to get up. While she pulled herself to the shower, I made a fast pot of coffee then, and moved myself to shower so I could perk up.

We both dressed in shorts and I slung on a tank top; Janet wore a halter and a pale peach top. She tied the tail up in a knot above her stomach. Hitting the hot air of New Orleans, we were immediately drenched by the humidity again. We agreed we were hungry so we took off to find an eatery. It was too late to eat heavy, so we opted for a sandwich and a drink. After our snack, we milled around with the crowds until about 11:30 p.m.

Thinking about the timing, I saw a man sweeping the sidewalk and asked if he knew where Hurricane's was. He looked at me with one of those "fuckin tourist" looks and asked me if I really wanted to go there; it was in Algiers. I asked if there was anything wrong with the area or the bar. He said, "No, not for me, but you just don't look the type." I thought because of the look he gave me when I asked about the place, he was being a smart ass. I puffed up and said, "What the fuck does that mean?"

He shrugged it off and told us to go south on Canal Street, then hang a right on Magazine. Go straight and then turn right on a street called Julia. It would be right there. As Janet and I started to walk away, I could have sworn he said "Midnight." I turned to confront him, but he had gone back to his sweeping. I shrugged and told myself I must be hearing things.

Janet and I started on our trek to find the bar. We wound our way through the people until we got to Canal Street. Following the directions, we headed south. The further we went, the more the crowd thinned out. The streetlights got fewer and the lights themselves seemed to shed a dimmer glow, the kind that throws long shadows. When we got to Julia Street it was almost total darkness. We thought for a moment we were lost. Then Janet saw Hurricane's barely discernible neon sign sporadically blinking. I guess I saw it too, but I was searching for a way to get the hell out of there if the need was to arise. I always look for an exit when I go into unfamiliar territory. Janet says it's left over from my mother's fright over a "roach motel" commercial. "They go in, but they don't come out." I think I inherited a cautious tendency from my father who always searched the terrain when we went hunting and he seemed always to know where he was and how to get back to the base camp. That area Janet and I were in on that strange night seemed just right for a hunt and we could possibly have been the quarry. I looked at Janet, she looked at me. I shrugged, she shrugged; we moved on.

As we approached, I looked at the entrance to the bar. An old weathered door with a handle like you'd find on a coffin, stood out when the sign blinked. I thought to myself, "how hokey was this." I pointed to the door handle and Janet gave me a halfhearted smile. I opened the door.

When I looked inside, for a second I thought I was outside again. A faint yellow light outlined the bar. A lone bartender had his back to the door. I didn't see anyone else as we walked up to the bar. The bartender didn't turn around so I said, "Excuse me." That's all I got out. The bartender pointed to the back of the room. I strained my eyes trying to see. I caught a glimpse of a lone figure in the corner. Janet gave me her hand and we walked toward the corner. When we were standing in front of this person, he gestured for us to take a seat. He stood and helped Janet with her chair. We sat. No one spoke. I watched this man. His movements were slow and somewhat exaggerated. I also noticed that he was still wearing his shades. I nonchalantly, or so I thought, reached to my right side and as quietly as I possibly could, unhitched the clasp on my knife sheaf, just in case.

Yeah, I carry a knife. As a matter of fact I carry more than one. I keep a folding *Buck* in a sheaf attached to my belt at all times. I also carry a *Gerber* folding knife in my left back pocket. That's on good days. When I'm at home, I carry five knives with me at all times. The two I just mentioned, two small pocket knives for easy work; I keep those in my front pant pockets and I sometimes have a blade strapped around my right leg. Wearing shorts doesn't make that practical, so I usually don't go strapped until the weather gets cold or I have to wear long pants to an outing. Janet says I'm paranoid. I like to think of it as (using a line from a Janis Joplin song) "I know this goddamn life too well." Knives are something else I inherited from my father.

The dark figure at the table reached up, pulled the shades down on his nose, and looked at me. The light was bad enough at the entrance, but here in the corner it made his eyes look blank, white, milky, and dead. He then spoke and in a quite tone said, "You won't need that here." Janet looked at me, then down at the knife and she punched me on the shoulder. I buttoned the sheath back and felt a little flush at being caught. I admitted to myself that I must have been getting old and slow. I've done that move a hundred times and never got snagged on it. Shielding my inappropriateness with bravado, I spoke up and asked him what he wanted, and what was up with this "one bone rattle stuff." I guess Janet sensed something then because she gripped my hand so hard, if it had been a piece of coal she would have had a diamond.

He spoke. "My name is Ceophelus T. Stringfellow. You may call me Ce. I practice a form of voodoo; some people call it white magic. I try to never cross over to the side where the devil waits. I use what I know to help folks see things, things that were, and things that may be. You want to know about the 'bone'. I'll tell you, but it has a price." At that, Janet squeezed my hand so tight again I thought she'd pull it off.

I said, "Okay, what might that be?" I was waiting

for a, your blood, or your first born, or your wife, something like that. I figured that after we all got over the smell of shit I'd probably dump in my pants, Janet and I would laugh all the way back to the condo. He leaned in close, and those eyes sort of rolled to the top of his sockets. In a low shaking voice, he told us it was a VCR.

The silence was at best brief. Janet broke the quiet with, "A VCR. What the hell? What do you want with a VCR, and how in hell is all this Dracula crap related to a VCR?"

The Ce guy rolled with laughter. He laughed so hard he held his sides so he wouldn't burst. I just sat there dumbfounded. Between his guffaws, Ce managed to get out "to watch horror movies." We all laughed at that comment.

The laughter slowed, there was a cough or two, and then we were silent again. Ce called the bartender over so we could order drinks; a Bloody Mary for him, a Sea Breeze for Janet, and a diet coke for me. When I ordered my "coke" Ce said, '*You take after your daddy.*' I looked at Janet, she looked at me; we both looked at him. He nodded as to confirm that we had heard correctly. I asked him what did he know about my father. He said he had known him when they were young. I asked him what else he knew. He shook his head, "*No. Not the right time,*" he said. "I want the VCR first." I sat there for a moment collecting my thoughts, then I looked at Janet. She gave me her, "whatever you want to do look."

I said, "Okay, one VCR. Are you sure there's nothing else?"

Ce said, "No, just bring the VCR to the St. Louis Square tomorrow, and then we'll talk."

At that point, the conversation dwindled to a stop. He asked me what time it was and I hit the button on my watch. Through the indigo glow it showed 2 a.m. I thought to myself, for two hours time had been running in slow motion or there must have been something in the drinks. I shook my head in disbelief. Ce said he had to go and I acknowledged that we did, too. I thought it was bad enough being in this bat cave, but getting back to our condo was going to be a real thrill.

We all stood about the same time. Ce reached out and grasped my left arm. I instinctively tried to pull away, but he held on. "What the----" was all I got out of my mouth. I saw his head go back like he was looking through the ceiling, in a far away, detached voice he said, "Be careful; these woods are full of monsters." At that, his hand fell away.

I felt as if a switch had been thrown in my mind. I could feel sensations of my past and my father's. Tiny prickly fingers ran up my spine. Ce turned and walked away into the darkness of the bar. I grabbed Janet's hand and we turned to go. At reaching the door, I looked back and there was just a dingy light above the bar; no one was there. I shrugged and opened the door. The humidity hit us. The heat even at this time of the morning was appalling. It grabbed us and crushed us with its heaviness. I began to sweat and something in the darkness of instincts intuitively told me to be afraid.

I told Janet to stay close and keep a sharp eye out. We began to retrace our steps back the way we had come. I looked at the buildings and the surrounding area with a keen sense of "I've been here before." A couple of blocks from the bar, the streetlights seemed to be brighter; but the light still cast long shadows along the buildings and into the streets. I saw the doors and windows of most buildings were barred or chained. Some of the doorways fell back into the buildings like the opening of caves.

We had just passed such a doorway when I heard something; something akin to the shuffling of feet. Janet pushed me forward by my arm and we quickened our pace.

I took a fast look over my shoulder, but I didn't see anything out of the ordinary. My eyes kept darting back and forth trying to see anything, anything at all that would spell danger. I turned my head to face forward. As soon as I did, Janet was pulled suddenly away from my arm.

I swung around to see her being flung up against a wall. Her assailant had his left hand pushed under her chin. In his right hand I saw the blade of the knife he had flipped out, a dull sparkle in the yellowish light. Seeing the length, I knew he had a banana knife; long, thin, and deadly. He kept his eyes on Janet, but quickly glanced in my direction. It was a hard look; he'd done this before. Usually there's a look of nerves on the perp in this type of robbery if the perp's new at it, and this guy wasn't nervous. He said, "Okay, mother fucker. I want your wallet, your watch, and the bitch's purse. Now! Now, or I'll cut this bitch to hell."

I was watching Janet. Her eyes were popping out of her head, and I knew this asshole was cutting off her air supply as hard as he was pushing her against the wall. He saw me looking at her and his ugly face turned to her's and he moved the blade closer to her chin.

I started shouting. "Okay, Okay, don't hurt her. My wallet's in my back pocket." I reached around to my right back pants pocket. At this movement, the asshole holding Janet jumped and when he did, the blade of his knife pricked her chin. She started screaming. At some point he must have seen the sheath on the side where I kept my "Buck." But he didn't see me twist the sheath downward and un- button the top allowing the Buck to slide out.

Our assailant started screaming also; screaming for Janet to shut up. I felt the familiar curve of the Buck in my right hand. I hollered that I had cash in my pockets and for him to please take it and don't hurt her any more. At that he said, "Hurry up, mother fucker, give me all you got." My left hand went into my left back pants pocket and instinctively found my "Gerber."

I said, "Please take these; please, just don't hurt her." The Buck opened as I brought my right arm around from my back pocket. The hilt struck him in the temple. He stood transfixed. His hands dropped to his sides and his knees buckled. Janet slid down the wall and sat down hard. I hollered, "ROLL" and she rolled away. With the Gerber in my left hand, I crouched ready to move in if the first blow wasn't enough to keep this pig turd down. I switched the blade to my right hand and went to Janet. Passing Lump on the ground, I kicked him. He was out. I quickly retrieved my Buck from the pavement, and closed the Gerber putting it back in my pocket.

I helped Janet pull herself up from the sidewalk and I quickly put her behind me. I looked around for any other punks, but he was it. I reached down and picked up the "banana" by the hilt. I saw an opening in the gutter for run-off and tossed the blade into the darkness. I positioned us under a streetlight close by and kept an eye on Lump. I looked at Janet's chin and gave her my handkerchief. For all she'd been through these past minutes, she held up great. I swung up and around to get Janet behind me and against the wall. I had heard footsteps again. I positioned myself to ward off any new attack. Crouched and ready, the sparse light outlined the silhouette coming toward us. I had the Buck opened, waiting. Janet made a half sigh, half start sound. The new member of this foray was none other than Ce. I relaxed to a degree, but still at the ready.

"One of the monsters wasn't so lucky tonight, I see," were the first words Ce spoke. He came up to the punk and poked him with his cane.

"That's for damn sure," I said, "damn sure." I shook my head in disbelief and then began to mentally beat myself up about what had just taken place. This punk came from out of nowhere when I was supposedly on my guard, and I missed him. Ce appears out of thin air and I "felt" him, and I was ready to fight. I asked myself if I were losing my grip on reality.

Ce looked around a second and then went to Janet's side. He moved her hand away from the cut on her chin. I was still watching him. It was either the light or the adrenaline rush, but I'm sure I saw his face draw back all at once and expose this harsh smile that showed teeth sharper than normal, almost canine. His tongue flicked out as though he was testing the air, like a snake does. In a voice barely audible, he said, "Take her and leave. I'll take care of this monster. Remember the VCR and bring it to the square at noon. Now go".

Ce quickly helped Janet away from the wall where I had her leaning. I took her arm and we began walking toward the condo again. I told her not to look back no matter what she heard. Something in Ce's tone had shaken me and I didn't want to find out why. It seemed like we were almost at a dead run when we turned a corner and saw a couple of people milling around the way lost tourists do when think they know where they are, but don't have a clue. Then we saw more and more people as we walked quickly. Finally we found ourselves at the condo.

We practically ran to the room. Opening the door, the cold air rushed out and hit us. As sheer comfort finally enveloped us, we knew we were alive. We both flopped down on the sofa. She grabbed my hand and leaned her head on my shoulder. I turned and raised her head to look at the cut on her chin. It was small, but red and angry looking. I gave her a kiss and rose to go to the bathroom to get a septic stick I kept for the times I cut myself shaving. I thought it would work on the cut under Janet's chin.

When I got back to her, she was fast asleep. Most people I know would still be so shaken from what had taken place, they'd be running for hours on the rush. Not my girl though. Extreme danger made her fall asleep when it was over. I guess it's a defense mechanism. She was at the point of hollowing out her eyelids with rim sleep. I ever so gently applied some of the stick to the cut. I then went to the doors and windows in the condo; the entry door, and the door leading to the small balcony outside the bedroom. I made sure they were all locked and chained. If I'd had a hammer and some nails, I would have hammered them shut. I made sure the windows were secure and took a couple of wooden coat hangers and wedged them tight against the bottom sash and the top of the frame for good measure. I went back to the sofa and squirmed in next to Janet. My mind and thoughts were gearing down from all the night's strange and harrowing events. My eyelids fell shut like they each weighed a ton and I fell asleep.

Chapter Three

Sleep is at best a thin film between reality and fantasy. As we lay there, my mind opened the doors of real memories and (what I suppose now to be) induced memories brought on by the night's events. These memories entwined themselves into a dream. I first saw myself a boy in Nashville. Having been, at one point, a "latch key" kid growing up in the Music City at my grandmother's house, with no key I might add. I used to stand in my grandmother's front yard in the afternoons after school and throw knives at an old hackberry tree. I threw at that tree for so long, I finally ringed it. It died and fell over during a storm. Watching these scenes unfold in my fitful sleep, I felt the exhilaration again of each thrown knife.

I then dreamt of myself wading a creek with a minnow sane scooping up shiners to bait trotlines and limb lines. There were pictures of wars, new and old. Countless deer ringing the tops of hollows. Big fish and little fish, trains, weapons, fights, jails, women, old things, new things, rushing by, over, and over again as though I was on a train, watching multiple lives rush past me.

Something startled me and I sat up in the bed. Beads of cold sweat ringed my mouth and forehead. Janet still lay beside me. Her quick little jerking motions told me she was having her own *bette noir* of strange shit occupying her. I tried to move away so I would not wake her, but my attempt was met with Janet grabbing my arm. I just said, "I stink" and headed for the shower. She looked at me with her, "let me first" look so I said okay.

She bounced from the sofa and asked me to fix her a drink. I hesitated. It was kind of early, but it was also our vacation, so I half nodded and went to the kitchen. I found the bottle of C.A.V., (cheap ass vodka) we'd brought with us and some cranberry juice. We had also brought some lemons and limes. I fixed her a mixture of C.A.V., CBJ (cranberry juice), and a twist of lime. As I was standing over the sink with the bottle of vodka held tight in my right hand, I caught myself raising the bottle to my lips with the intention of taking a long, hard swig. An old voice in my head said NO! I put the bottle down, picked up the drink for Janet, and took it to the bathroom.

I opened the bathroom door and the steam from the hot water of Janet's shower rushed out to greet me. I went in and sat the drink on top of the commode tank next to the shower. Then, I sat down on the john and closed my eyes for a second. Janet's hand moved the shower curtain back just enough to poke her head out and see me and the drink. Reaching for the drink, she asked me if I had made myself one. I said no. She took a sip and said she didn't know how I did it, especially after what we'd been through. I just shrugged. I thought to myself how Janet enjoyed a good drink and held her liquor with the best of them while I was a flake when it came to drinking.

I learned the hard way that old man K'hol controlled me no matter how I fought to control him. I used to listen to the stories that the old people in my family would tell about my father and the things he'd done under the influence and how his father reacted to drinking. I, of course, lied to myself in my youth and gave myself the ol', "it'll never happen to me; I'm too strong" speeches. All that shit was a bust.

The shower curtain opened again and Janet's coquettish voice broke up my pity party and she invited me to join her in the shower. There's nothing like a good shower to clear your head. There's nothing like a good shower when you're with someone you love.

After we were out and dry, we went and stretched out again on the sofa. The cold from the air conditioner and the warmth from the shower woke us up; something like a sauna and a dip in a cold pool. As we lay there, my mind turned again to the previous night's events, that is until my stomach growled. I knew we had a date with CDM coffee and some beignets. I looked at Janet and slipped her a kiss. I told her of my hunger and she responded saying that she was famished, too. We looked at each other; possibly a second went by until we literally jumped off the sofa, hurriedly dressed, and took off to the market.

After we spotted a table surrounded with shade, we sat down. Even though it was early and usually at this time it should have been cool, the heaviness of the humidity brought the promise of a suppressing, sweltering day ahead. It took a few minutes before the waiter came and took our order. Even though I stared a hole through him, he didn't "shift" as it were and I was certain it was going to be an easier day. Sipping coffee, we sat there and talked about the strangeness of yesterday and last night's events. I kept an eye on the different types of people walking past. My sense of danger was peaked due to last night and I wanted to be ready if somebody decided to infringe on my day. Our order came and conversation dwindled. We found not talking, but savoring every bite and sip of our fattening treasures, was what was called for in that instance. I looked at Janet from time to time and thanked God he'd given her to me. Without her, I'd be doing time somewhere or I'd be dead. She was my focus.

Janet and I met right after I came back from the "promised land" aka California in '72. It had been a promise alright. I had moved out there after high school in '69 with hopes of being more than just another *Nashville cat.* When I got there though, I soon found out that I was lumped in with the other wannabe's. After nearly starving and having no real place to live for months, I found a job! I worked twelve hours a day in a clay pipe factory near San

Bernardino; nothing but dirt, heat, and sweat. The money was good though, and I was finally fitting in to the *culture*, so I hung in there.

While I was *fitting in*, I had met a little girl, Trimania, one Saturday night in June of '71 at a local watering hole. She was of Spanish decent and when I first saw her, she pulled my trigger! As luck and time would have it, we started getting close. When her old boy friend found out she was hanging with a gringo, he decided to *save* her by killing me. I honestly tried to stay away from him, but he wouldn't have it.

One Friday night, we ran across each other in the parking lot of the local taco palace. I talked a blue streak to get this guy to see reason, but it didn't do any good. The more I talked, the madder he got. Trimania tried to talk to him, and she got a hard slap for her efforts. The situation was cool until that moment. When I saw the blood rush from her busted lip, I went into what I call the "red rage." It's sort of like the Viking mentality, when those guys would go berserk in battle. I cut that boy literally a new asshole and then some. One of the bystanders called the cops and I was arrested. He was rushed to the county hospital and made it through the night. I sat in the local jail for a week. The locals couldn't get anybody to press charges; honor among combatants I guess. Anyway, I was told to "get out of town" and I did. I went back to Tennessee.

I met Janet a few months later in Nashville and my life has been pretty sweet since then. We met at a buddy's house one night. His wife knew Janet when they were in school and had arranged a surprise supper for us. The surprise was, we didn't know the other one would be there. Our relationship bloomed pretty fast. We had, and still do have, what's known as *chemistry*. When we became more comfortable with each other I told her about my "red rage."

I knew she thought I was blowing it out of proportion until the day we were in a situation where it reared its ugly head.

We were leaving a mall in Nashville and as we were headed out of the parking lot, a car from out of nowhere cut across a number of parking places and slammed into us. Janet had bounced up and hit her head on the windshield. The pressure when she smacked the glass made her head bleed. All I saw was the blood. Janet said I flushed bright red. I slammed on the breaks and literally jumped from our car and ran over to the other car. When I looked in the other car, I saw some clown laughing so I grabbed him and pulled him through the window. All I saw was this buffoon and didn't even realize I had reached across the car and pulled him out of the driver's window from the passenger side and had drawn my knife called a "butterfly." It's a knife with a handle that opens similar to a butterfly and exposes the blade. I reacted so quickly as in a single movement

I was holding him up with my left hand and getting ready to pig stick him when Janet came up behind me and said, "No! Put the knife down." I stood there with this guy kicking and screaming in my left hand and my lungs sucking in air like I was pumping billows at an iron foundry. Janet said that she put her hand on my arm and just looked me in the eyes and the color began to show in my eyes again. She told me later that when she first saw my eyes they were solid red. After I totally calmed down, I found out it was his girlfriend that was driving not him. Both of them were stoned; that's why he was laughing. Somebody called the cops.

The police came and an eyewitness told them I had a knife. During the wait and the crowd gathering, I had slipped the butterfly into the tail pipe of a car. When they searched me, I was clean. They searched our car and Janet's purse. No knife was found. Unfortunately, the car with my knife in the tail pipe drove off, and I can only speculate what happened to it. After this incident, Janet has kept a watchful eye on me and has helped me learn to control my anger…well almost.

The waiter came and asked if we needed anything else and that broke the spell of the memory I had recollected. I took a quick glance at my watch and saw it was almost 10am. I told Janet we needed to find a "Wally world" or a "Kwal" and get the V.C.R. I asked the waiter if he could point us in the right direction. He told us where the closest department stores were. The Wally world and Kwal were about 20 miles from where we were. We thanked him. I paid the check and then we left the restaurant and caught a cab to the department store of choice, Wally world.

As we road toward the department store, Janet and I both sat in silence. She knew that anything I ever find out about my father sets me off. I grew up seeing him on weekends and some holidays. Mother and he were divorced soon after I was born. When we were together, we went fishing and hunting and he taught me how to use the knife. He was difficult to know in any other aspect of life. When I was young I thought it was because he was shy. My grandmother told me stories about him and I blew them off because when I asked him about the incidents she had told me, he would brood and say nothing to me for a long time. As I got older, we grew apart both as family and confidants. When he passed away in 1984, I looked at a corpse of someone I really didn't know and it still bugs the hell out of me. So if this guy, Ce, says he knew my dad, I want to hear what he has to say. Janet lets me have my way on things like this. She doesn't question my motives or my hunches. If this vacation went to hell because of the encounter with Ce, well, I guess I would have the devil to pay to make things right.

We arrived at Wally world in about 20 minutes. Getting out of the cab, I told the driver to wait for us. Going directly to the electronics department, we quickly looked at their selection. They had a 4 head, bare minimum unit on sale for 97 bucks, so we bought it and were on our way to the square.

Chapter Four

Sometimes life is easy, you know? Then other times it's like a pile of tangled coat hangers. Well, we got to the Square about 11:15 a.m. and thought for sure we'd see Ce setting up his table. He wasn't there. The area around his "place" was empty. It was as if there was an invisible rope around a 3 foot by 3 foot space and none of the other people who used the square would cross over that line. The sun was really pouring out some heavy rays by then and with the humidity, man, you'd think water would sweat in that heat.

Janet and I looked around the Square over and over again, but no Ce. I asked a woman who set up at the right of Ce's spot if he would be there today. She looked at me and giggled. She shook her head; first yes, and then no. Then, she shrugged her shoulders and didn't say a word. I was just about ready to go when Janet nudged me. She said she was going to go and get us something to drink. I gave her a kiss and told her to be careful.

When I turned back to Ce's area, in the middle of his space sat what seemed like a lump. Actually it was a little old man with a grocery sack. The way the light hit the concrete and the way he was all scrunched up, he sort of looked like a lump. The local church bell rang. It was noon. He raised his head. I found myself standing three feet from the deadest looking eyes I'd ever seen. I stared at him for a moment and then I asked him if Ce were coming. He told me, no he wasn't.

His voice sounded as if old stale air was pushing through a hollow tube. Ce's absence and rudeness made me mad enough to blow a gut and I was just about to let loose with some words that would make a sailor blush, when the little old man spoke up again. "Mr. Madison, Mr. David V. Madison." The anger left me. I stood there like a house of cards and if there had been any sort of a breeze, I would have fallen over onto my face I answered and he stood up. His thin dark features seemed to float toward me. The heat was playing with my eyes, I guess.

He stood right in front of me. "I'm Snid," he said, extending the sack toward me. I asked what was in the sack. He explained, "What Mr. Ce had you buy that V.C.R. for, video tapes." I gingerly took the sack and looked inside at the contents. He was telling the truth; inside the sack were a number of videotapes.

I looked at the messenger and said, "Thanks, but why didn't Ce come himself?" He smiled or I thought he smiled. His lips were so thin his teeth were almost showing through them, so it was hard to tell.

"Mr. Ce ate too much monster last night and when he does that, he has to rest awhile." I thought to myself that either this guy was a nut or old Ce was playing "this" tourist for a sucker and carrying it as far as he could.

"Okay. And I suppose Mr. Ce wants me to give you the V.C.R.?"

He shook his head no and declared, "How will you watch these…" pointing to the sack, "if you don't have the V.C.R.?" I stood there somewhat dumbfounded.

Janet nudged me again as I turned around and she held a cold drink out to me. She inquired if I had heard anything from Ce, yet. I held up the sack and opened it to show her the tapes. She asked me where they came from. I nodded my head toward the "lump", and kept looking in the sack. Janet spoke up and asked me what I was trying to show her. I swung around and did a quick survey of the area. I stood there stupefied. Lump, as I called him, was gone.

The seemingly ridiculous, but cryptic events really pissed me off. I was looking at Janet and asking her what kind of lame shit were these people trying to pull on us, as though she had the answer. I had a new V.C.R. and a sack full of video tapes and the only person who had given me any answers about anything was nowhere in sight.

Janet suggested we go back to the condo to see what was on the tapes and stop trying to figure out crap that was too spooky to deal with in the hot, open daylight. I spoke to point out that if this guy was so hot with his mumbo jumbo, how is it he couldn't see that the condo had a V.C.R.? I shrugged my shoulders as if I was answering myself. All I could get from my own question was a "fuck if I know." We took off back to the condo.

On the way, I told Janet we needed to get some blank tapes so we could use the condo's V.C.R. and the new one in tandem to copy whatever we would find on the tapes that might be of importance to us. She agreed and we stopped at the local drug- store and found tapes on sale. At least, I told Janet, this vacation wasn't costing us too much, Ha! She hit me. Picking up a pack of legal pads and some #2 pencils, she chuckled that with our luck we needed to write as much of this stuff down as we could because something spooky might happen to the V.C.R. Janet had taken shorthand in high school and used it in college to take notes in classes. It was a skill she kept honed by using it in her daily work. During meetings she'd write down "important" concepts and base her staff memos accordingly.

We hurried from the drugstore and wound our way through the sweating masses back to the condo. Again we thanked the heavens for air-conditioning. After being out in the New Orleans oven, I took a whore's bath, washing under my arms and putting on fresh deodorant so the stink from my pits wouldn't drive us out of the condo. Besides, I still had work to do. Janet hit the shower. I went to the living room and began setting up the V.C.R.s in tandem.

When Janet came into the room, she had fixed us a

big pitcher of fresh lemonade and we sat down to watch the tapes. I hesitated and held on to the one designated as #1. Hesitating, I got up from the couch and began pacing back and forth in front of the TV. Janet finally told me, after I'd worn a rut in the carpet, to either do it or don't do it, but make up my rabbit ass mind. I took a deep breath and put in the first tape, then the one to make the copy. I sat down on the couch again. Janet had her pencil and paper at the ready. I took a big swig of lemonade and sucked in a lung full of air. I hit PLAY on the remote and began the first tape from Ce, then hit RECORD on the new V.C.R.

The image we first saw was of a room with antique furnishings which gave the impression that it was some sort of drawing room like one would see in the old period films. In the back of my mind I was thinking of how hokey the room looked. This image stayed on the screen for a few minutes. During that time, I kept looking back and forth to Janet. After a minute of the still image, she told me to quit looking at her; she didn't know any more of what was going on than I did.

With a slight smile, she reached over and gently turned my face toward the TV screen. We heard a noise coming from the background of the tape. It sounded to me as if someone was clearing their throat. A figure walked in front of the camera and sat in a chair that faced the lens. It was Ce. He had a walking cane with him and when he sat down, he did it with the practiced grace of a person who was old and infirmed. He positioned the cane on the floor next to the chair, then he crossed his legs and placed his hands on his lap. He looked straight into the camera. A silence fell. It was so loud you could hear the static in the tapes as they played.

With no warning he spoke, "David." I sort of jumped when he said my name out loud like that. The voice was strong this time. I could not resist sneaking a quick glance at Janet, but she was glued to the screen, her hand moving the pencil across the page of the legal pad.

I am, Ceophulus T. Stringfellow. I was born on Friday the thirteenth; 1914. I am of the Stingfellows of Beauray Parish, Louisiana. We are distant cousins. I will not fill the ensuing hours of this narrative by droning on about every nook and cranny, the climatic conditions, or anything else I feel will hinder your imagination. Exploring the different facets of a life are not all cut and dried; so, I will at my own discretion, emphasize the parts that stand out. I am going to impart to you a story of your father, his life, and his death. I know you have heard some of these remembrances before. What you will hear from me will be the truth. I will begin this narrative about your father before he and I met. I will first tell you how it was for him in his native Tennessee. This story is for you so you will know your father; it is your story too *when the bone rattles.* I wish I could relate all this to you in person; however, an old malady keeps me from coming into too much contact with people. On a good day, or night, I can spend a few hours with those who can withstand my presence, as we did the other day and evening.

You remind me a great deal of your father. Your eyes show his strengths and his weaknesses. But enough of this chit chat. Let us begin.

Chapter Five

David V. Madison, your father, was born on November 17, 1917. His name is your name. (I shot a fast look toward Janet at this statement.) That's right. You have the same name as your father's. For many years I know you were told that you were named after a man your mother was in love with, a lawyer of all things. The truth is your mama was seeing this creature while she was married to your father. When your father found out about this unseemly liaison, he divorced your mama. The courts though, favored mothers in those days.

In Tennessee, even if the mother of a child was the spawn of Satan, she would get custody of the child. Dick was your father's nick name. Clarence Edward, his sir names, were added when your Grandmother Bessie legally had his name changed. I'm going to tell you now what really happened.

Ce slowly closed his eyes and from where I was sitting on the sofa I didn't know if he was still breathing. The pregnant pause stretched to the point an elephant could have been born. I found myself inching forward closer to the TV.

To start, let me say that your great grandfathers hated each other. (I jumped back from my forward perch. This renewal of the narrative continued as though he'd never missed a beat.) There was bad blood between them. Money and whiskey both played in that cat box. The story goes that at one time, these two were thicker than thieves, if you will. They ran stills and sold whiskey all over Tennessee, as far east as Knoxville and as far west as Memphis. Many a small town depended on their enterprise.

Now, old Mr. Madison had a head for figures and

could turn a dollar, while Mr. George had a head for building and setting stills so revenuers could not get to them. They also had an uncommonly loyal group of runners and customers. They were quite the entrepreneurs.

They say that money has a way of seeping into a man's blood. It's like a poison. It can kill a man slowly; kill all he loves, and those who love him. Madison began to skim more and more money from the operation. He took this money and bought up most of the county where they lived making sure to buy as many local officials as he could, too. The sheriff, the county judge, and anyone else he thought would benefit him in his pursuit of owning a kingdom, came under his purse.

George spent a good deal of his profit on materials to make better whiskey in hopes of going legitimate at a later date if the prohibition was ever lifted. After a heated argument about cutting the cost of making the whiskey by using shoddy material, bad sugar, and old corn, George finally made Madison fess up to what was going on. Blows were struck, weapons were drawn, and blood was spilled. They were such a good match, they could not whip each other. Both were as strong and versed in fighting as the other. The partnership dissolved with hatred for each other. But as fate would have it, just like in Shakespeare's play--if you know *Romeo and Juliet*--their children, Bessie and David, found each other and fell in love or heat, and married. The children went to Nashville and got a ceremony performed by a justice of the peace. The hatred the patriarchs had for each other spilled over into the lives and times of the family members, especially for Bessie and David, your grandparents.

Mr. George, your grandmother's father, to spite his enemy, made your grandmother change your father's name from David. V. Madison to Clarence E. Madison. He threatened to take her out of his will if she did not comply with this unreasonable, heartless demand. He knew that changing your father's name might push Madison to the great beyond a little faster. Now, your Grandmother Bessie, your father's mother, despised both of these old reprobates for controlling her day-to-day, seesaw life. Bessie did what her father demanded, but to get back at him, she decided to nick-name your father Dick, a neutral name. Neither the George's, nor the Madison's could draw spite from Dick. That's the name that stuck and that's what people called him all his life. You may be wondering why his father didn't intervene. What you just heard was family recollection. What I am going to impart to you next is taken from what I have personally seen.

Ce's voice trailed off at that point. I thought he was going to take a break or something. Instead, he leaned his head back, then forward and down. Shortly, his head rose slowly and he looked at the camera again. His eyes were gone. Not like missing; but like drawn up in his head and all you could see were the whites. I looked at Janet and she was sitting there with her mouth open. I suppose I was, too. Ce started talking again as though he was far away and talking over time.

The light from an old coal oil lamp pushed its way through the grimy window pane in the kitchen. It managed to throw odd shadows on the hodgepodge of boxes and trash strewn on the back porch. One of the distorted images was Dick as he huddled next to the back door. He slept outside the house during the summer. The nights were cooler. You might say the outdoors was his bedroom. His momma made him a small pallet by the door.

On this night, though, he was not asleep. He rubbed

away the tears and snot that ran down his dirty face onto his arm and felt the welt on his cheek his father had given him with his razor strap. Always keeping it nearby as a cruel idea of discipline, his father used it like a bullwhip on Dick and his mother when the drink took over.

Tasting the salty blood from the busted lip his father had also given him, he spat it out onto the porch decking. He could hear his mother screaming and his father cussing. "You damn Georges think you own the world, but you don't own me. I'll kick your old man's ass if he fucks with me too much."

"Oh! David, please don't be this way. It's not daddy's fault. None of this is anybody's fault but yours and that whiskey you swill," Bessie screamed at the drunk standing over her. Dick heard the sound that hard flesh makes on soft flesh when his father slapped his momma. He cringed. His mind raced with fear and hatred for his father. He knew what he wanted to do, he wanted to grab hold of his father's raised hand and shake the drink out of him, but he also knew he wasn't big enough to do it yet. His father started that drunken behavior when Dick was younger, about the age of six or so. He was ten years old now.

David started working at a local sawmill and farmed, too. Along with the constant badgering he got from his father and Bessie's too, David turned to whiskey. Mr. George would give Bessie a little money to keep herself up, but threatened to cut her out of his will if anything went to David. David's father threatened him with the same scenario if any of his money went to Bessie. David and Bessie were caught in the middle.

David and Bessie loved each other at first but, as they say, "money is the root of all evil," or better yet, it was the constant reminder of the young couple's "lack of money" being pushed down their throats that proved too much for them. The relationship quickly rotted and festered until the poison poured out by two old enemies found love's roots and killed David and Bessie's marriage. When David would draw his wages from the mill, he'd get drunk, come home, and abuse Dick and Bessie physically and verbally. Dick had tried to stop his old man from slapping his mother around, but he was too small to do much at ten years old. Dick only aggravated the situation when he tried to help his mother. He would get slapped, too and catch the hot end of the razor strap. His momma would hurry him off to the back porch, and he would wait until his old man fell asleep and rolled around all night in his whisky piss. Too often he would shit himself too and leave the mess for Bessie to clean up. When she thought David was asleep soundly, she would go to the back porch and try to soothe Dick's pain, the internal as well as the external. Mostly it was the external. He would try to soothe her as much as a child could soothe the pains of an adult. Holding each other, they sometimes fell asleep together.

Not that night though. That night new sounds drifted on the slow breeze. The woods' sounds. A frog croaking louder than usual, a fox screaming so loud that it sounded like the life was being scared out of some young girl, the chirping of a cricket so loud Dick thought he was sitting on it. The smells that wafted in on the slow breeze were warm and moist and full of night jasmine and honey suckle.

While Bessie held him, rocking him back and forth, she thought he would fall asleep as he usually did and tomorrow would come bringing a possible reconciliation. This night however, Dick's attention was aimed at the woods and what his senses told him awaited if he would run to them. He knew these woods well. Every deer trail, fox lair, squirrels nest, and gopher hole. If it lived in these woods, Dick's woods, he knew about it. He had hunted and trapped these woods since he was four years old. His father showed him a great deal of what he needed to know before the drink stole him from Dick. Everything else he had learned, he learned from the school of hard work and perseverance.

He slowly removed his mother's arms from around him and stood up. The poor light was mercifully hiding his resolution to be gone. "What's the matter, Dick?" Bessie asked. He wiped the tear streaks from his face and in a sad voice told his momma that he had to go. He couldn't stay around any longer and see her mistreated and not be able to do anything about it. He wasn't going to run off for good. He'd come see her; but not him, not his father, not until he was big enough to handle him.

Bessie began to cry and sob. She pleaded with him to stay. Things would get better, she promised. He placed a hand on her head, leaned down, and gave her a kiss on the cheek. He then whispered to her, "You are my heart. I will love you always." She broke down into heaving sobs. Tears welled up in Dick's eyes. He wiped them away as fast as they appeared. "Bye" is all Bessie heard next and Dick was gone. His barefoot quickness left her alone as though she had been talking to herself or to a spirit. She didn't hear Dick leaving. All she thought about at that moment is *why her*? Why did she have to suffer so much. It wasn't her fault she had to do what her husband wanted and what her daddy said for her to do. Otherwise, she'd be penniless like he told her every time he saw her. She couldn't bear the thought of that. Dick was a good boy. Bright and eager to learn, he'd be all right. Sure, he would.

Her mind went from that thought to David and the mess she'd have to clean up. She was so rattled the last go around, she forgot to move him from the bed and he beat her for letting him wallow in his own filth. She moved quickly. Maybe she could get him up and in a kitchen chair so she could wash him and then strip the bed and wash the bedding. If she could do that, she could hang it on the line and it would be dry before noon. David would let her get by with that. He wouldn't miss Dick tomorrow. Dick usually disappeared for a day or two after one of David's drunks anyway.

This would work out just fine and she wouldn't have to hear David's harping or hear about her father when he came by for his visits. David was usually at the mill when her father came by. Everything would be alright for her. A thin smile came across her face as she got up from the porch and went inside the house to start working her plan. Anyway as long as David was passed out he couldn't yell or beat her.

Dick ran. Dick ran fast. He ran through the woods in the darkness as if it were broad daylight. He cleared the downed trees, the low branches, and the webs the wood spiders had spun in the dwindling light of the day. His eyes, accustomed to the dark, allowed him to discern the deer paths and fox runs that his feet now followed. Run. He had to run, run as far as he could from his drunken father and his mother whom he could not protect. One day though, one day he'd show his father he was man enough to take the strap from him and stop the drunken abuse toward his mother and him.

He was getting tired now. His lungs were sucking in the cool night air so fast he thought his ribs would break. The anger that drove him into the wood was waning. His thoughts were becoming scattered. The pumping motions from his arms and legs had served him well enough, but now they were aching from the strain of the running.

Errant thoughts led him back to his school where he had competed once long ago and had shown he could run with the best of them. He had won a ribbon for beating the other boys at recess on the day they had intramural competitions. He even beat the older boys.

Watching the deer and the small creatures run during his short years, he had fitted his movements to theirs which gave him a distinct advantage over the normal running. Every muscle was in harmony with the others in his body. He had taken the ribbon home and had given it to his mother. She was so proud of him. When she told his father, he shrugged. "So what, can that damn ribbon pay for anything?" Remembering the incident, his anger flared again. He sped up. He closed off all the sounds around him. If his eyes could have been seen by another human, they would have shown bright blood red.

His aching muscles screamed for him to stop, and stop they did. Instinctively, he jumped an old log near the spot where he was heading. When his feet hit dirt, his knees gave way and he was propelled forward, landing face first and sliding on the dew covered weeds to a quick stop.

He laid there, his lungs heaving so hard, they sucked dirt into his mouth. The smell of crushed milkweed along with an assortment of small gnats and flies were sucked in as well. Pushing himself over on his back and reaching out to grab onto the huge log, he was able to get into a sitting position. Wedged snuggly against the thickness of the log, the body wanted to give in to the exertion. His lungs were still heaving from the efforts. His right arm, feeling like it was made of lead, made his hand move to his mouth to wipe the mess away. After cleaning his face, the deadweight arm came away from his face and plopped on the ground next to his body, immolating his left arm. His head fell forward and his chin rested on his heaving chest making him look as if he were saying yes to questions posed to him by some unseen interrogator.

He may have dozed, he didn't know. Upon regaining composure, he looked at the sky, studying the stars, and guessed that it was about midnight. He tried to push himself up from the ground. It seemed the weed-carpeted floor of that part of his woods would not let his body break the bonds they had formed with him. His arms, legs, and hips all strained to the point he felt pain, but he persevered and with a hard grunt managed to muster up enough strength to get up. He stood swaying for a second when, like a giant friend, the log caught his falling body and in essence held him up. He took a long, deep breath and almost screamed when his lungs expanded. He coughed and spit up some bile, then wiped the spittle off his mouth. With another painful gulp of air, he pushed himself away from his steadying post and took a few steps forward. His favorite spot to sleep in the woods was just ahead. A few steps and he would be at the entrance and sleep in comfort, with no razor straps. Dick's strained body let his mind wander and his overtaxed muscles pushed him forward one step at a time, then he'd hesitate and sway with the night's slow breeze.

Closing his eyes for any moment, his mind would grab onto a memory. This time it was about his friend, Bad Eye and how they had found Dick's favorite place. He unknowingly smiled, his body swaying and jerking as it tried to move itself forward. They'd been running traps the previous winter and had cut through this part of the woods to get to the "Tunnel", a favorite summer swimming hole. This place was ripe with the muskrats they would trap during the season. His thoughts drifted further remembering when Bad Eye lost his left eye.

On a cold, dark December morning about three years ago near his huntin' grounds, Bad Eye was checking his traps along the stream when the ice near a bank gave way. As he was hurled, falling head first into the stream, his left eye caught onto a short stem of frozen water grass. He ended up losing it altogether. It didn't seem to bother him none, though. He was still a crack shot, able to read, and to cipher. As far as being called Bad Eye, that didn't worry him none either, it was a badge he wore proudly 'cause he had earned it. Anyway, if anybody thought less of him because of it, in those times and in that place, no one said anything out loud.

Bad Eye actually found the place that became "their" place by stepping through a rotted board and almost breaking his leg. He screamed when his leg went out from under him. As he was in mid-stride when the solid earth vanished, he found his left leg under his chin and his right leg suspended in up in the air but still under him. Dick was a little ahead of Bad Eye and on his right. When he heard the scream, he swung around in a crouched posture and had his fist ready for whatever was coming.

Sizing up the situation quickly, Dick raised himself to his full height. He stayed on the right of Bad Eye and moved toward him. When he got within a few feet, he saw what had happened. There were plenty of old wild grape and muscadine vines hanging in the nearby trees. Dick went and pulled on some that were suspended from a branch near where his friend was hung up. Bending the branch into a bow, Dick told Bad Eye to grab hold of the vines when he got close enough. When he got near enough, Dick yelled, *"Now!"* Bad Eye grabbed hold of the vines the way Dick had told him.

Now, Bad Eye was a couple of years Dick's senior and a foot taller, but Dick outweighed him by 20 pounds. When Dick let go of the vines, Bad Eye shot out of that hole like a cannon. The vines whipped on the end of that branch with Bad Eye holding on with all his might. It looked like the tree had caught a live one. When they became taut, the sound of the vines snapping was like the sound a small caliber bullet makes when it's fired. *POP!* At that sound, Bad Eye knew it wasn't being slung that would hurt, it would be that sudden stop when he hit dirt.

When he did slam onto the earth, Dick ran up and rolled him over. Bad Eye just lay there and moaned. Finally after a few seconds of prodding from Dick, he got to his elbows. Looking at Dick with a pain induced grimace, he said, "If I'd known we were going to beat me to death today, I'd have stayed home." Dick roared with laughter.

Dick helped Bad Eye stand up. Holding on to Dick's shoulder, Bad Eye limped over to where the hole was now located. He looked at it for a minute and shook his head in disbelief. Dick told Bad Eye to sit down and he'd look at the leg that went through the hole. Both boys wore overhauls and it would be easy for him to roll up Bad Eye's pant leg. There weren't any large cuts, but his shin was scraped right well. Dick went off, leaving Bad Eye sitting for a few minutes by himself. When he returned, Bad Eye had dozed off in the afternoon sun, snoring like a big frog. Dick laughed just loud enough to awaken Bad Eye. He was carrying a hand full of muggwart and creek mint mixed with mud. Both boys knew the combination of the two would keep the scrapes from festering like the old folks said. Dick rubbed the mixture onto the scrape and covered it with fauns from a fern. He then tied the poultice into place with some twine he kept for making trotlines.

When this was done, he helped Bad Eye up from the ground. They started walking so the muscles in the injured leg wouldn't start cramping. Curious about the hole, they moved to where Bad Eye had taken his spill. Dick got a long stick and tapped the ground in front of him and Bad Eye, the stick acting as a sounding rod and a depth finder. The closer he got to the hole the tapping began to make a more hollow sound. They stopped.

Dick looked at Bad Eye and told him he had an idea. He would pull some vines from another tree then tie them around his waist. He told Bad Eye to let the vine out slowly, but hang on to it as he moved forward. If the ground gave way, Bad Eye could keep him from falling to the bottom of whatever the hole offered. Getting to his knees he moved forward from where he and Bad Eye had stopped. Along the way he dug in the ground with his hands and found another board like the one Bad Eye had unearthed, then another one, and more as he went along. He removed as much dirt as his hands would allow and finally told Bad Eye they'd need a crow bar and a shovel to complete the job. Bad Eye said he had both at his house. It was getting late though and he was feeling stoved up, so he opted to bring the bar and shovel the next day. Dick said okay. Helping Bad Eye back to where they had met earlier that day; they parted, wondering what they had found and figurin' it was keepers for them.

Each of the boys slept little at first that night, their minds conjuring up tales of lost treasure and underground storerooms full of loot the Yankees had taken from the South during the altercation between the states. Dick's thoughts settled down after a while with the realization that what they would probably find would be nothing. Sleep overtook his mind eventually and he didn't miss a wink.

The next day, Bad Eye found Dick waiting for him at the hole. Bad Eye had brought the crow bar and shovel as promised the night before. He could tell his friend was hot to get to work by the way he was fidgeting. Dick grabbed the shovel and jumped into removing the dirt. When he had gotten all he could from his vantage point, he told Bad Eye to start removing the boards. Bad Eye jammed the crow bar into the board he had fallen through as close to the end as he could. All he got for his effort was another hole in the board. The rotten end of the board wouldn't allow the crow bar to get a bite. With shovel in hand, Dick went around the exposed board and jammed the point of the shovel into the ground until he found a spot that was all dirt. Looking around, he spied a rock the size of a softball. With one hand and foot, he pushed the shovel into the ground. Once this was done, he placed the rock as close to the shovel blade as possible. With a deliberate motion, he pushed down on the handle of the shovel and leveraged the back of the shovel against the rock. His pushing finally made the old board and the loose earth around it come up just enough to get a hold on it. Quickly, he reached down and grabbed the board dropping the shovel. He heaved with a grunt. When the board began to move under his exertion, it made a squishy sound like the earth was trying to suck it back to its resting place, but Dick prevailed. The old board gave as Dick twisted it left and right, then he gave it a pull. Plop! The board was out.

Dick stood there a minute and looked at the board, then Bad Eye. He motioned for Bad Eye to come to his side and when Bad Eye came 'round, Dick did the shovel trick again. This time with Bad Eye helping him, another/ stubborn board popped out in a flash. They took all of 15 to 20 minutes to clear the whole area. From his figuring, Dick guessed the hole was just about a 9' x 10' opening. They could almost see the bottom. Dick wanted to make sure there was solid ground in the bottom so he looked around and found a stone, a big stone. He and Bad Eye pried, dug, and grunted. They got the stone out of the ground and with one boy on each end, they picked it up and took it to the edge of the opening.

Taking a deep breath, they both slung the stone out as far as they could toward the center of the hole. It fell and fell fast. In a second or two the stone hit bottom. They thought they would hear a plop or thud, but what they heard was a big stone hitting a bigger rock. Crack! Dick grabbed the vines he had used to maneuver around the hole, re-tied them to his waist and used a big one from another tree close by as an anchor rope. He walked to the edge of the hole, looked down, then swung around at an angle with his ass

hanging out over the expansive space that intrigued him.
He let himself down through the cleared opening.
When he got to the bottom he looked around, he was
surprised to see and feel that the bottom of the hole was, for
all purposes, dry. The bright sunlight of the morning hadn't
found its way over the rim of the hole yet or through the
tops of the overhanging tree canopy, but in the shadows of
the light that he did have, he caught a glimpse of a door.
Upon this discovery, he hollered for Bad Eye to find some
pinecones, young ones with lots of sap. When Bad Eye had
the cones, he hollered and Dick told him to put one of them
on a stob and lower it down to him. This done, Dick told
Bad Eye to come on down.

Dick untied himself and let the vine rope flap
against the wall of the hole. As soon as Dick's weight was
not putting tension on the rope, Bad Eye began to pull the
rope up the wall as fast as he could. As the rope moved, it
looked as if an Indian fakir was blowing a flute to a fast
tune and his magic rope was leaving the hole of its own
accord. Dick saw Bad Eye skinning down the wall with a
big smile on his face. "What did you find, Dick? Old civil
war stuff, skulls and such? What?"

Dick nodded toward the door. Bad Eye looked in
the direction of Dick's nod and if his face had lit up any
more, it might have caught fire. He walked over to the door
and for some reason knocked. Dick laughed. "Boy, you
ain't right." Bad Eye returning Dick's laugh said, "If any
body had answered with 'come in', I'd have been out of
this hole in a shot." Dick snickered at that and took matches
from his overhauls, struck one, and lit the cone. It blazed
and gave off a pine oil smell. Bad Eye had brought 4 or 5
cones stuffing them in his pants pockets. It made him look
like an oversized chip monk with a winter's supply of nuts
to store.

Dick told Bad Eye to hold the torch and pulled on

the door handle expecting it to be rusted tight. It was difficult, but it began to open. The boys heard the air rush in through the small opening made from the initial effort. Getting another foothold, Dick pulled harder at the door. With the torch still in one hand, Bad Eye managed to get a grip on the door and helped Dick push. They got it open enough for both of them to squeeze in the opening at that point. The first pinecone torch was just about burned out, so they hurriedly affixed another one to the stick, lit it, and went in.

The room had a stink of old things, almost like the smell of a skunk after it sprayed with most of the odor washed away by a good rain. The light from the torch fell on old wooden boxes, a table, and cobwebs. The floor and walls were limestone. If they had entertained any thoughts of finding treasure, neither boy let on to the other that they were disappointed. All they found was an empty room. Bad Eye said to Dick that it was a bust. Dick answered Bad Eye that it was a boon. They could fix the place up and no one could find them if they didn't want to be found. It could be their place to hide or hole up if they were trapping and the weather got bad.

During the course of the summer, the boys worked at cleaning up the "skunk hole" as they started to refer to it. Bad Eye brought a coal oil lamp. Dick was able to come up with some poles they strapped together with vine to make a couple of bed frames. The old table was a little rickety, but it held up. They replaced the boards over the largest part of the hole overhead. Dick spread the dirt back over the boards. They left a spot just over the door where they could slide down into it. Eventually, they made a ladder by lashing cedar saplings together with vines, a sort of roll-up ladder. They knew they'd have to re-lash it from time to time until they got hold of some rope, but that would work for the time being. Finally they pieced together a safe house they could get to when the need arose.

They both had come across a small fuel can and by the end of summer, they had pilfered enough coal oil to fill the can and keep the lantern lit for a good while. The inside of the room was sparse, but livable. The bed frames were covered with pine bows and Bad Eye had come across a three-legged chair. They stuck a piece of one of the old boxes they'd found under the corner of the chair where the leg was missing. It was wobbly, but it worked. Both boys brought can goods when they could. The temperature, they noticed, was neither hot nor cold, but it was bearable. The lamp put out a little heat when they were there, but it felt OKAY to them.

It was Okay, Okay, Okay! Dick's mind flung itself back to the boy that had managed to half drag himself to the edge of this sanctuary. He pulled at the branches he and Bad Eye had attached to a piece of canvas and this exposed the opening to the "skunk hole." A darker blackness reached out of the hole up to Dick, but he knew it held no threat. He lowered himself down into the opening, his feet swinging in the blankness until they found the ladder. Every aching muscle in his body strained as he let himself down. As he lowered his body slowly with what little strength he had, he pulled the cover back over the hole. The sounds of the woods faded and he was in total emptiness. His right foot touched the solid floor, then he was standing there swaying from fatigue. If one could have seen him then, he would have looked as if he were swaying to some unearthly melody. He sucked in a large amount of musty air and the volume expanded his lungs to the point of pain. He coughed hard. The pain slapped him out of his stupor and he moved again. Bending over to get the lantern from underneath the old box, he grunted.

He raised the lantern glass and reaching into his pocket, fumbled for a match. Finding one, he pulled it out of his pocket and struck it across the wall he knew was in front of him. It looked like a tiny tracer shot from a tiny cannon exploding into a blue yellow flame. The light the match gave off hurt his sight a little bit, but when he lit the lantern his eyes tried to push their way to the back of his head in an effort to get away from the brightness.

Through the tears that formed, Dick found the door and pulled. At first he thought it was stuck, and then he realized it was him, his strength was all but gone. He set the light down and with a grunt of frustration, the door pulled open, but only a little. He picked up the light and mashed himself through the opening. He took a quick look around and stumbled toward the more familiar bed. After he sat down on the bed where he always slept, he lifted up the lantern glass, then blew out the light. He almost dropped it as he put it down on the floor. He tried to swing his legs onto the bed, but he couldn't. He just let his upper body fall back and as soon as he hit the soft bedding he let out a sigh, which almost sounded like a death rattle. The darkness made his blanket, the silence tucked him in. He slept.

Chapter Six

Ce stopped talking. A shadow came across the screen. The little man, Lump, hesitantly came and stood beside him. Ce slowly said that he was going to take a break. We could either fast forward or take a break ourselves. I had looked at Janet from time to time as she was writing and every so often she'd shake out her writing hand. I knew she was getting cramped so we opted for the break. About that time, snow filled the TV screen. I took the controls and hit STOP at the same time for both units. Janet and I both let out a sigh of relief and anticipation.

I looked at my watch and showed it to Janet. All we had consumed that day was a pitcher of lemonade, and this "hoss" was hungry. I told Janet we needed to saddle up and head for the chuck wagon. We didn't think about stocking any provisions when we had first arrived. She put down the notebook and stretched like a cat. She said to give her a minute and off toward the bathroom she went. I walked over to the window and peered out.

Out front, the rue had filled up with the usual mob of people. All they did was mill up one side of the street and down the other. I didn't see anyone without a drink. Na'lens was totally different at night. That's when the titty bars were all open and the street freaks were out in full. I do not like crowds! I do not like being rubbed up against by people. I shuddered, but I knew I was going to have to hit the streets again. After what happened the other night, I was, to say the least, gun-shy.

Janet came back into the room, pulled me away from the window, and told me we'd be alright and to remember, Ce had said we were going to have a good time. I said OKAY and checked to make sure all my knives were where I could get to them then checked for my wallet. It was there, my shoes were tied, and I had on matching socks. I was ready, except for one thing, my wife. She gathered her purse, made sure she had her can of pepper spray this time, and we were off.

The sweltering heat of city was just what I needed to get me to the point of hurry up and get back to the condo. We maneuvered through the crowds and Janet got a Hurricane. I opted for a tall, cold diet coke with lots of ice. There are many wonderful restaurants in Na'lens and every one we went to was as full as it could be. An hour wait was usual at most of them. We went to several and finally settled for Owen Brenin's. While we were crammed into the bar area like sardines, I tried to order a drink for Janet, but the bar staff was so busy, I wasn't heard over the noise around and behind the bar.

Time, when you are hungry, can be as slow as crap. We finally got a table and our waiter tried his best to accommodate us. I ordered the lightest thing on the menu I could, so I wouldn't gorge myself and fall asleep when we got back to the condo. I had a Caesar salad along with peel'em and eat'em shrimp. Janet had an ettoufe and lobster. She ordered a glass of house wine while I ordered a Sharpe's non-alcoholic beer. We ate and talked about what we had heard that day. We were relaxed, comfortable, and filling ourselves to the brim.

Ce was right in his assessment so far. I had heard snatches of what he had related today from some of the family as I was growing up in Nashville, but not in the detail he had given. Sounded like old grandpappy needed the shit kicked out of him. I don't remember him at all. I remember Bessie a little. I could see in my mind's eye an old lady with a dribble of snuff coming out of the left corner of her mouth and asking me for a kiss. Gag me with a spoon, nasty. I shook this memory off and we talked about Bad Eye and his role in my life. I knew old Bad Eye when I was growing up.

I remember the day I first met him. My dad had taken me and my brother fishing for the first time with Bad Eye in tow. It was down on the Harpeth River outside of Nashville near a place called the Tunnel. I caught my first fish with Bad Eye's help when I was only 4 years old.

I reflected also about the day Dad and I found him dead. He was old by youth standards, in his late sixties. He had been living in a cabin above the Harpeth near the bridge on Highway 70 west. Bad Eye's niece had called Dad to tell him she and her husband hadn't seen him in a couple of days and wondered if Dad had heard from him. I was at Dad's house when the call came. When he hung up the phone, he put his hand to his heart. He knew Bad Eye was gone.

Before we left to drive down to the cabin, Dad got some oil of wintergreen from my stepmother, who we called Ma'zell,. I remember her stroking his cheek before we left, no words said between them. When we arrived at the cabin, Dad took the spare key from under the special rock by the stairs going up to the front stoop. It was a slow climb that day. When we got to the door, Dad took the oil of wintergreen and put some on our handkerchiefs. He told me to hold it under my nose. I didn't do that at first, but when he opened the door, the smell of death liked to have knocked me down and I started gagging. Dad put the snot rag under my nose and in a second or two I was okay.

As always the cabin was neat as a pin. Bad Eye may have been country, but he was one of the cleanest men I'd ever known. We went to Bad Eye's bedroom and saw him lying in his bed as if he were asleep. The bloat had taken hold and he looked as if he were pregnant. I almost fainted. Dad grabbed my arm and kept me afloat. He told me to use the phone and call the sheriff, they'd do the rest. We waited there and when the sheriff came, he brought the local coroner. Dad called Bad Eye's niece and they both broke down over the phone. The funeral was small, just us and his niece and her immediate family. Dad and Ma'zell sprung for the coffin. Bad Eye was buried next to his mother.

Janet tugged on my pants leg and said I was taking one of my trips again. I said I was sorry and explained I was thinking about Bad Eye and Dad and Ma'zell. Big, fat, heavy, tears rolled down my cheeks. Janet called me a baby, nicely, not poking fun. She reached over and dried my tears. I don't know why, but when I get to thinking about all the ones that are gone, I get funky. Janet said to finish up and we'd go walking around to get this maudlin feeling out of our vacation. I agreed and we called the waiter, got our check, and bugged out.

Back in the midst of all the wretches, I thought, didn't these people have lives? Couldn't they have all gone to Disney World? Why did they have to be here pushing their nasty bodies past mine? Selfish, I reckon. Sometimes my phobia of not liking crowds made me think stupidly. Duh! Janet was having a good time though and I put my bullshit aside for a while.

You know, sometimes you get a feeling that someone is watching you. It starts up the crack of your ass and slowly moves up your spine. Like the hain't in an old Vincent Price movie I'd seen years ago. Somebody was watching us. I popped the buttons on my scabbards. Moving closer behind Janet, I told her to get her spray ready, something was going down. I literally got a feeling. Someone stuck their hand in my back right pocket where I usually keep my wallet. I reached around as fast as I could and grabbed skin. I heard a "let me go" from a voice that was deep and angry. I pulled the individual from behind me and to my surprise, it was a little boy about 6 or 7 years old. I looked for Janet and she was still walking ahead, so I hollered for her. She quickly turned and had her spray in hand. I smiled at her and laughing said, "Look what I caught." I was going to let him go, but out of his little mouth came a barrage of filth that made me blush. I told Janet to see if she could spot a cop and I'd hold on to "happy boy." He stopped cussing and started kicking me in the shins so I snatched his other arm and held him in the air as far away from any special targets he may have tried to attack. In a few minutes after kicking didn't work, he started hollering for his daddy. Janet said she saw a cop and she'd go get him. The crowd around me parted to some degree and I suppose the *man-mountain* that pushed his way through was the person he was calling "daddy. "

"What the hell are you doing to my kid, asshole?" were the first words from biggun's mouth. I said, or tried to say I had caught him trying to lift my wallet, but "daddy" took a swing at me and I had to duck. I was still holding on to the little fellow and ducking daddy's attempted breakage of my jaw. The crowd made a ring of sorts and I guess if I had been a bystander this would have looked funny to me, too. He'd swing at me, I'd swing at Jr., and the dance would start all over again. I heard a "move aside" coming from the center of the crowd and finally "John Law" and Janet broke through the peepers.

"Alright, what's going on?" he intoned. I tried to get a word out to explain the pickpocket, but daddy kept on coming. The cop told me to let the little boy down and back off. I unceremoniously dropped the little shit and as soon as his feet hit solid, he booked. Daddy saw the cop the same time "fleet foot" took off and he suddenly got very docile. The cop stood between me and daddy. Daddy started off with a barrage of "this guy was abusing my kid, I want him busted." The cop looked at daddy and in a "don't bullshit me, buddy" tone said, "Look, that 'kid' was no more yours than I am. You don't recognize me do you, Harry? "Harry" stopped in mid-sentence and looked real hard at the cop. "Officer Hobart, I didn't recognize you, but now I can see you plainly. My anger has gone down now. This 'tourist' was manhandling my boy, Terry." Officer Hobart held up his hand to old Harry. He didn't even have to say, "talk to the hand" and Harry shut up.

The officer looked at me and asked me what happened. I told him how I'd felt something in my pocket and it turned out to be this Terry. He asked me if I still had my wallet and I said yes. He also wanted to know if I wanted to press charges against old Harry for aiding and abetting a known pickpocket. I said sure, why not. He said ok, but the perp and Harry would be back on the street in a few hours. It was Mardi Gras weekend and the jails were full of drunks and stoners. I said, "Then, why ask me"? He shrugged his shoulders and said, "It's part of the job." I thought for a moment and said, "Let's forget the whole thing, OK?" Janet and I started to walk away but Hobart said to hold up. "Now folks, just to let you know, its also part of my job too, that Terry is not a little boy, he's a dwarf. He's 20 years old and has sometimes been known to carry a weapon, usually some sort of pig sticker. If you see him again, be careful, he may want to exact a little revenge on you." I thought about that comment for a moment. If this little shit was as bothersome as Hobart had said, why wasn't he calling for back-up to look for this creep? The mind is a horrible thing to waste, the saying goes. I think Hobart flushed his down the cynical toilet early on in his career. I told him I'd be watchful and if anything else happened or we saw Terry, we'd call the police and let them know. He did a two-finger salute off the brim of his hat. We turned and left the area.

Hobart moved back to talk with Harry and a new set of on-lookers crowded in to see the blood and gore, if any. We moved away as fast as we could. I told Janet that if this was fun and exciting, shoot me next time. She giggled and said that everything would be okay.

We found ourselves at the French Market and strolled through the stalls looking at the unique jewelry, foodstuffs, and the regular tourist trinkets. Janet picked out a ring she found interesting and I saw some alligator tail meat that was being touted as the world's best. I asked for a sample and the counter person cut me a small piece. I popped it in my big mouth and it liked to have burned the lining out. Janet said I turned twenty shades of red, sweat pored from my face, and my booty tightened up big time. I bought and drank a six-pack of water in nothing flat. Janet kept acid reducers in her purse for me so I chewed two of them and we found a seat for me. Man, that was some piece of hot tail, no pun intended. I guess the gator was laughing its head off in gator heaven. I love having fun.

After this episode, we decided to head back to the condo. Janet said it wasn't safe being out with me. Ha! Ha! We picked through the masses and headed back along the avenue. I thought I was going to throw up or something. I had a sharp pain in my gut that bent me double. I put out my hand to steady myself and that feeling of being watched came over me again. Janet was propping me up and I told her something was up again. She looked at me hard and said, "Will you please stop this paranoid stuff about being watched? Sometimes expecting the bad makes things happen." That was a true comment.

About the time she finished saying that, I saw a small figure run around the bushes near the side entrance to the park where we'd stopped. I had in my mind it was Terry, but it could have been a small child running just as easily. I sat for a minute and the pain in my gut subsided. Feeling better, I said let's move on. Janet helped me up the best she could and we started out again. I heard small running feet coming up behind us. I pushed Janet away from me and swung around. Janet almost fell, but caught herself on a lamppost. A child ran past. As soon as I turned to meet the onslaught, a glimmer of blade moved my instincts into action. I did a double butt, throw back, suck your gut in, bullfighter's pass with the hands. The front part of my shirt had a long cut across it. I yelled at Janet to roll. She hit the ground running and never missed a beat. Her pepper spray was out and ready. I guess the "razor imp" didn't want any of that so he ran back toward me.

A loud retort filled the silence of the moment as the thunder of a shot rang out. The boy didn't know what hit him. He was dead before his feet knew it, nevertheless he made a couple of extra wobbles, but the bullet had torn a hole in his spine and the bone fragments punctured all his vital organs. He collapsed in a heap and then he fell over. People scurried for cover and I heard whistles being blown like the cops use. Janet ran over and I pushed her behind me up against a tree. We were facing the open area.

Within a few minutes the police came. Officer Hobart was the third cop on the scene. Janet and I were pulled to one side and the two cops that arrived on the scene kept an eye on us. Hobart came up to me and asked for the gun I used to shoot Terry. I said, "Whoa there, sunshine. Thanks for asking about *us!*, and yes we're fine. Really, we're just great." I told him there wasn't a gun. He spoke to me in a flippant tone and again asked me where the gun was I used to shoot Terry. By this time, I was getting pissed and asked him, "Are you deaf or just stupid? I've told you, WE DON'T HAVE A GUN, you twit." He stood there a second. Then he managed to get out under his breath a command to "cuff 'em." Bad move on his part. I cannot, and will not voluntarily relinquish the ability to move my arms about. I am, for better or worse, claustrophobic.

Janet spoke up and told him, "You really don't want to do this." He told her to be quiet and motioned for a couple of cops to move in on me. One grabbed my right arm, one grabbed my left arm. They pushed me against a cruiser and pulled my arms behind me. That's all I remember for a good twenty minutes. I went blank. When I came to my senses, I found myself being held at bay by cops with M16's and I was bleeding from a cut under my right eye. I looked for Janet and couldn't see her. I opened my mouth to call for her and one of the guards stuck a barrel in my face and told me to just shut up and stand there. I felt fucked. I felt like I'd really done it this time. I stood there a few minutes searching the crowd for Janet. Her voice came to me. Damn the guns, I called for her.

Officer Hobart and Janet came past the guards. She grabbed me and gave me a hug and a kiss.

"I tried to warn them about your claustrophobia, honey, I really did. But, before I could tell them anything about how you react to being hemmed in, it was too late. You went into one of your rages and that's all she wrote. You wore the three of them out in nothing flat." She whispered into my ear, "I tried to get you away before you did any knife business, but it wasn't fast enough. That Harry guy came up and in the confusion, started to swing on you, and you sort of cut him. They've taken him to the hospital to get sewn up. I explained all this to Officer Hobart, honey. He's made some calls and it seems they know Ce. We can go back to the condo until they get word on Harry. God, I hope you didn't kill him." I took a quick look at Hobart and saw a nasty bruise around his left eye. He was staring at us like we were the "tourists from hell," dabbing at his eye with a handkerchief. Hobart told us he'd send someone by later to get an official statement from us.

God! God! God! I don't remember anything that happened during the blackout. I stood there blank faced. I guess I looked stupid, I don't remember. I do remember walking away. Hobart stopped us. "Don't leave town" is all he said. I stared hard in his eyes. The reflection I saw showed hate and fear mixed. I knew I was screwed. He pulled away and gave me a two-fingered salute off his hat.

As we approached the condo, my head cleared enough to ask Janet if they knew who shot the kid. She said, "They still think we did it. I think it would be classified as self-defense but…" she shrugged. I then asked her about the cops I assaulted. She said, "Wait until we get inside". I thought that was a grand idea.

We got to our door, I found my key, and we went in. The cold air from the AC wrapped around us with friendly intimacy and I think both of us sighed at the same time. We walked into the living room and sat down on the sofa. My shirt was still open in the front and when I sat down, the cool of the air ran its fingers deeper into my body. Janet told me to take off my shirt and she'd look at the neat red welt that now ran across my mid section. I stood up and walked over to the mirror hanging by the fireplace.

"Damnnnn. That little fuck almost did the number on me. Look at this." Janet came over and gently ran a finger across the thin road map that now ran the expanse of my gut. She sweetly told me to go shower and when I finished, she'd put some ointment on it the way I did for her cut. I kissed her on the forehead and went to shower.

I was clean and somewhat rested, sitting back on the sofa when Janet answered my question about the cops. She said that as I was being pushed down across the hood of the cruiser, I belly flopped and mule kicked the cop who had my right arm. When he dropped to the ground, I rolled to the left as the other one stood there blank faced, and "ippon nukitaed" him in the throat. While he was gasping for air and the other one was holding on to his swollen jewels, I managed to hang a half nelson on Hobart and had drawn my Buck. She said that's when she stepped in. I started calming down and in a few minutes I was breathing easier and that's when the "swats" showed up.

Janet told me they were getting ready to "pop a cap in my ass" when a big wig told them to stand down and let her handle me. She said she kept up the reassurances and it was like flicking off a switch. I put the Buck up and let Hobart go, and then I just stood there. That's when the "swats" took over and the guards were positioned around me. The rest I knew. I lowered my head and cradled it against her lap. I said in a somewhat muffled voice that one day she wouldn't be there and I'd be a dead fool. She patted my head and gently kissed me on the ear. I stayed in her lap for a few minutes then I shook it off; the feeling of impending doom drained away.

I sat up and said, "I need some coffee." She had fixed coffee and mentioned something about food. I told her that whatever we were going to eat, it would have to be delivered because I wasn't going outside again until we were heading toward home. It was too much having to deal with the victims of "cervical rubieosus," (red necks) and the "rooster fish" police, (cock suckers). Giggling she said, "Amen." I slugged down some coffee. She called for pizza. I was now ready to watch some more of the tape.

I took the remotes and pushed the magic buttons to get the ball rolling again. I fast-forwarded the tape until the room appeared again. I saw Ce come into the room and sit down in the chair. His "little buddy," Lump, was in the background. I watched him move around as Ce prepared himself for the next phase of the narrative. Lump had something in front of him. It looked like a stick. I could barely see him while the camera was positioned the way it was, but to me the stick looked like the barrel of a rifle. I reached over to Janet and said, "Honey, look." I pointed to Lump and the corner. Ce was getting ready to start talking. I pushed stop on both systems. I hit REWIND on the controls and watched in reverse motion the scene that had unfolded before. She leaned forward and I hit PLAY. The movements I had described to her were there again. She took her pencil and notepad to write this down as a "question to be asked." Did Ce have anything to do with the shooting of the pickpocket? In my mind I told myself that if Ce did have the Lump whack the little freak, more power to him. He saved my life.

We were so intent on watching Lump, that we both jumped when Ce began to talk again.

"Well, we're back. I hope each of you is feeling alright and I agree that it may be better for you both to stay within the confines of the condominium. You've by now realized that 'Mr. Snid' took care of the situation you've just returned from. I received a message about the *pest* from my friends at police headquarters." Listening to Ce's comments, I thought to myself how professional the hit on Terry had been.

"Yes," Ce, broke my train of thought, "Mr. Snid' is a crack shot. I'll tell you more about him another time. I think it's now prudent that we get back to the narrative about your father."

I hit STOP on both controls. I shook my head at Janet and she fell back into the sofa. "How the hell did he know what just happened tonight, if this tape was already made before today?"

Janet said something about a scam. An elaborate hoax of some sort to get us in a bind and we'd end up paying out the ass for all this. I smirked. Pay what, all our millions, sell the yacht, and all our stocks? She agreed we were a pretty bad risk if anyone wanted money from us. She was scared now. Crap like this just doesn't happen, you know. She was drilling me about why were we getting involved with all the voodoo shit, and all the stuff about my father could be bull shit, too. I thought about what she had said to me for a minute and I reached for the phone.

I started dialing and Janet asked me who I was calling. I told her, my Aunt Jenny. If anybody knows if this is true, it will be her. She made it her business to keep a pulse on us. The phone rang three times before Aunt Jenny answered. "Hello," she said.

"Hey girl," was my reply. She knew who it was when I said that. We traded pleasantries and cutting to the quick, I asked her if my dad had ever been in Louisiana. Aunt Jenny had always been the family historian. If anybody wanted to know anything about anybody in the family, they would ask Jenny. There was a pause and then she explained, yes, as a boy he had gone to Louisiana for a time with an uncle on his mother's side. A Johnny Potts, if her memories were correct. We had not heard anything about Johnny yet, but just her mentioning dad having been in this part of the country sent a shiver up my spine. I "zoned" for a second and when I came back to earth, I asked her if she had ever heard dad say anything about anyone named Ce or Ceophelus.

Again there was a moment, then her voice came over the phone so loud I pulled the receiver away from my ear. She did that sometimes, shouting over the phone, especially if she knew you were calling long distance.

"Yes, that name was familiar. Ce is a name your daddy referred to when he would talk about his boyhood friends. Why are you asking about this David? Why this sudden interest in the family lore?" I told her that I ran into a man named Ce, who said he had known dad and zzzzzzzzzzzzzz.

The phone went dead. "Hello, hello?" The buzzing of a disconnected phone was all I got. I hung the phone up and told Janet that the phone went dead. She crinkled her brow and asked if I was sure. I reassured her all I could hear was a buzzing sound." She got up from the couch and came over to where I was and picked up the phone. She looked at me, holding the phone out to me saying, sounds good to me.

"Okay. My bad." I must have hit the disconnect button. I shrugged. "Would you please call Aunt Jenny back for me while I get us some coffee?" Janet began dialing the number and I went for the coffee. Bringing the cups back into the living room, I saw she was standing there with a puzzled look on her face and the phone just hanging in her hand.

"What's up?"

She looked at me and said there was a recording that stated the number we dialed was out of service. "See," I said. "I told you it went dead." She then reported the recording also said that the connection had been down for approximately a week and that's why no calls had been going through.

"Bullshit, I just spoke to Aunt Jenny not 5 minutes ago and ..." I shut up. Then I said, "Okay, Okay, let's not get squirrelly. Let's just sit for a minute and drink our coffee and sort this out rationally."

Well, that was a bust. We sat for a long minute and said absolutely nothing to each other. I sat there thinking, the more weird shit happened, the easier we were letting it slide. Janet spoke up and said we just needed to get back to the tape. I said, "Sure, why not?" I hit the controls and the tapes began again; one recording, one playing. Ce's face filled the screen.

"As I was saying, I think it prudent that we get back to the narrative. Please do not cut the machines off unless you need to take a break and at that time please say so out loud." I looked at Janet and saw the fright in her eyes. With that, I resolved to end this mess. "Please don't be afraid. I

have, as your generation likes to say, your backs covered."
I looked at Janet again and this time, her hand and pencil
were going full blast. I calmed down. She would let me
know when she had had enough.

Ce sat back in his chair again. His head fell back,
forward, and then back again. His voice began again to tell
of Dick's seeming demise.

Chapter Seven

Dick awoke. His vision was blurry due to thickness of the grime stuck to his eyes. He spit on his fingers and rubbed the sockets until he felt the cool air of his surroundings hit his opened orbs. He knew where he was. He just couldn't remember how long he'd been there.

The young boy slung his legs to the side of the bed, his feet touching the floor. He sat for a moment and then reached for a match. Groping in the darkness for the lamp, his fingers found it. He pulled the chimney glass up and reached down to strike a match along the floor. The tiny sparks hurt his eyes and made him squint. When the match got to full flame, he moved it toward the lamp making the match look like a falling star. A soft hue covered the room at first, then a bright yellow light from the lamp filled the small room.

In an effort to see how he felt, Dick shook his head and tried to stand. The pain shot through his body, all his muscles rebelling at the same time. He tightened his ass muscles to keep it shut or he would have shit himself, he hurt so badly. Pushing down on the table, he steadied himself and stood up. His lungs were sucking the damp air in and when he had gotten enough, he held his breath as he moved. Gingerly, he walked to the nearest wall and reached for it. He let out the breath. With his arms extended, he let his fingers inch up the wall until he had his arms fully above his head. The effort made him sweat. He put his forehead against the wall, then. With a wheezed grunt, he flipped himself around and slammed his back against the wall. He almost passed out. Standing there shaking, Dick caught himself and slowly inched down the wall until he felt his ass touch the floor. Then he proceeded to push himself back up the wall. He did this moving his arms up and down until he worked the kinks out of his body.

His stomach roared loudly to let him know he was hungry. He went to the shelf where he and Bad Eye kept a few cans of pork and beans and peaches for emergencies. He took a can of pork and beans and sat down at the table. He licked his lips in anticipation of tasting this treat when it dawned on him he had no way to open the can. Dick lowered his head and rested it on the table. His mind was blank. His eyes shut and sleep overtook him again.

A familiar voice in his head awoke him. "Dick? Dick boy, you down there?" It was Bad Eye. Mustering up strength and pulling in enough air, Dick managed a squeaky "yeah." Bad Eye literally jumped into the "skunk hole" and pulled open the door to see Dick sitting at the table staring at a can of pork and beans. Bad Eye asked if Dick was alright. Dick just sat there and pushed the beans forward with his nose. Bad Eye took out his homemade knife and pushed the point of the blade into the top of the can. Then, he see-sawed the blade around the can until the lid could be opened. He pushed it back over to Dick.

Attempting to use his right arm again, Dick winced when he moved it just to have it flop down onto the table. He inched his hand to the can and picked it up. He put the rim to his mouth and let the beans, pork, and juice poor into his mouth. He made a half-assed effort to chew, but most of the can's contents were just swallowed. When the free flow stopped, he asked Bad Eye for his knife and finished off the rest of the meal by using the blade like a spoon.

Dick spoke to Bad Eye between gulps of food and told him what had transpired the night before. Bad Eye told Dick that he had gone over to get him a while ago and Dick's mother had told him he'd run off. Bad Eye told Dick that his mother said it was OKAY for him to come home now. Dick gave Bad Eye a look and Bad Eye shut up. Dick explained that as of that day, the "Skunk hole" was his home. He declared he would see her when he could.

"Well, old hoss," Bad Eye said, "if you're going to hole up here, we'd better get you set up proper."

The resilience of youth took over as the day wore on and the aches and pains that plagued Dick worked their way out of his system. Dick remembered a saying he'd heard once: "Pain is God's way of making weakness leave the body." He knew he was going to be strong as badly as he had hurt. That evening before Bad Eye left, they picked "Jewberrys" and "muskeedines." They'd found some sassafras root and had boiled it to make tea. Eyeing the make shift larder their days work had provided, Dick knew he was set for a day or two. Bad Eye and Dick exchanged a quick glance. And with understanding, Bad Eye went home.

Dick spent the next few days scrounging around the areas where Bad Eye lived. Some of the things people had thrown away found their way into the "skunk hole" and the boys began to make a real "palace" out of it. It wasn't junky though, everything had a place. Dick had found an old butcher knife that had been broken and the blade was only about four inches long, but he took it anyway. He worked the blade on sand stone and rounded it to a point, then he honed the blade sharp.

Dick watched his house one morning until his father went to work. A few minutes after his father left, Dick worked his way to the back door. He let himself in through the screen door. His momma was upstairs cleaning. Dick went down to the root cellar by way of the trap door in the kitchen. Moving the small throw rug that covered the trap door, he opened it. His momma would hide things there and one such item was his old 4-10 shot gun. She had hidden it there once after Dick had threatened to use it on the old man during one of his bad drunks. Dick knew where it was; he'd known for a pretty good while. He took the gun and the two shells he had kept with it. When he got back up to the kitchen, he put the weapon outside by the kitchen door, moving in the room as quietly as a soft breeze so his momma wouldn't know he'd snuck the shotgun from its hiding place. He came back to the trap door, and closed it, then he replaced the rug. Walking back to the screen door, he flung it open and let it slam shut, then he hollered for his mother. The sounds of her activities quieted. "Dick, is that you?" a strained voice said.

"Yes, Mama. It's me." Dick stood there and heard the floorboards on the stairs squeal as his mother made her way down to the kitchen. When she saw Dick, she rushed toward him, then abruptly stopped as she saw him back away. Wringing her hands in the apron she had on, she looked at Dick and he looked back at her. The time between talk was short after Dick blurted out a hello. That broke the thin coolness of the moment and the guards of distance between them fell away. Dick's mama came up to him and pulled him to her and gave him a hug. He just stood there. He wanted to hug her back, but he couldn't. He told her that he was okay, and he'd decided to stay away for a while. He'd bring her some money as soon as he could.

The thousands of questions he hoped she wanted to ask him never came out of her mouth. When Dick mentioned money, she allowed herself to fall victim to her greed. "It'll be your money momma, and you can buy things for yourself. Sweet boy, she said.

Turning away from him, she went to the breadbox and took out a couple of slices of bread. She lifted the dishtowel that was covering a plate of left over pork chops and put one pork chop between the slices of bread. Unthinkingly, she handed him the sandwich and set about wiping down the table in the center of the room.

"Son, do you know how much you'll bring me when you come?" his mother asked.

"I'll try to bring you some money once a week if the hunting's good and I catch enough fish. Mr. Barton at the store said he'd pay me 10 cents a piece for the rabbits I brought him and 5 cents a fish."

"Bring me what you can, son. I saw a new hat in the Sears catalog I want." "It never occurred to Dick to ask her to get him anything, just so long as she was happy everything would be all right.

The days and nights of that summer passed as they would. Dick was doing what he loved for the mother he loved. On the weekends, he'd get close to his house and hear his old man swearing loud and his mother's sobs. All he could do was disappear in the woods.

Dick and Bad Eye made the summer in the skunk hole. Bad Eye would stay the nights as he could. His momma wanted him home after dark because she was afraid that he'd get hurt and lose his other eye, His father was in no way the drinker old man Madison was and he wanted "Thurman" (Bad Eye's' real name), home at night because that's the way families were suppose to be, together.

Bad Eye didn't mind the pork and beans, the fresh fish, or the occasional rabbit, but he liked his mother's cooking the best and when there was enough he would bring some to Dick the next day. Dick knew Bad Eye had told his folks what had happened to him. He didn't care. The Griffins had always been nice to him and Bad Eye was the truest of friends.

That fall, Bad Eye's father died in an accident at the sawmill. A chain, used to strap down a load of logs on a truck, snapped and cut Mr. Griffin almost in half, from his neck to belly. There was a closed casket funeral. Dick was there. Bad Eye's mother sobbed and occasionally let out a scream. The mill wives, her friends, gathered around her and tried to console her. Dick's mother made an appearance at the funeral home and signed the registry, but his father was nowhere to be seen. Dick stayed at Bad Eye's side during the trek to the cemetery. The preacher said words about Bad Eye's father, and the people dispersed leaving Mrs. Griffin, Bad Eye, and Dick by the grave site.

Mrs. Griffin stood there and watched as the gravediggers filled in the hole. Dick watched her and Bad Eye and saw the resolution of finality on their faces. Mrs. Griffin said out loud to no one in particular that she needed to get back to the house and start packing. Bad Eye looked at her and asked what she meant by that. She told him that the mill owned the house and neither Bad Eye nor she worked at the mill, so they had to move. Bad Eye looked at Dick, and Dick saw the youth drain from his friend's face.

A few days after the funeral, the two boys met at the "hole." Bad Eye told Dick that his maternal grandfather had told his mother that they could have a couple of acres and an old house near the Harpeth River over in Cheatam County near a place called Whitebluff and that's where they were going to move. The two reflected on the stories they'd heard about the Harpeth and how, during the Civil War or "troubles" as their folks would call it, old John Bell had moved slaves up north along the river near an iron foundry he'd built. Bad Eye was excited to be going, but sad that he and Dick wouldn't be able to be close any more.

As darkness fell that day as the boys sat across from each other. The long shadows began to disappear and silence loomed in the "hole." Dick broke the quiet with uttering one word, "Well…" Bad Eye returned it with his, "Well…" They moved to the entrance and climbed up the rope ladder. It was to be Bad Eye's last climb up that familiar ladder. He stood there looking down into the chasm that had been his sanctuary, too. Dick stood looking at his friend and finally said, "See ya."

Bad Eye turned and took off through the woods back to the house he'd called *"home"* all his life. Dick moved slowly through the woods toward his house, a place he'd called *hell* all his life. He was alone. He saw the dirty light from the kitchen pour out into the blackness of the night. He was like someone transfixed while dying, staring at the light before the other life begins and this one ends.

Chapter Eight

A couple of days after Dick and Bad Eye left each other at the "hole," Dick watched Bad Eye and Mrs. Griffin get on a wagon that held all their belongings and start their trek to Whitebluff. Dick hung back at the end of the wagon as it started down the road. Bad Eye looked back at his best friend and as the wagon sped up and moved away from Dick, Bad Eye gave a half-assed wave goodbye to his friend. Dick didn't wave back. Dick had resolved to himself that life was hard early on. Bad Eye wasn't dead, he'd just moved. They'd always be friends; there wasn't any call for caterwallin' about it.

Dick steeled himself about Bad Eye and kept his mind on the situation at hand. School was to start soon and he was not in the mood to sit in a classroom with a bunch of smart-ass kids learning things about nothing he knew he'd ever be apart of, and as far as he was concerned, the only "practical" thing in school was the arithmetic. For his age, and grade level, he out-performed a number of older kids.

Everything stopped. The screen filled with static and video snow. I stopped the second recorder and as soon as I hit the button, the supposedly "out of order phone" rang. Janet and I both reached for it. She, being closer and faster, picked it up. I watched her face as she said hello and she kept looking at me while the other party talked to her. I sat there pulling at her elbow, whispering, who is it? She pulled away and turned her back to me. I was left with trying to hear some of the conversation, but I only picked up a "sure we'll be there." I was beginning to get irritated.

Janet hung the phone up and stared, zoned for a minute like she was in disbelief. I again reached up and touched her elbow and that broke the zone. She told me we had to go to the morgue and identify a body. Immediately, I wondered why we had to identify a body and then, stared at Janet.

"What, who the hell was that" I asked. It was Hobart Janet responded and she explained the police had gotten another body and they wanted to see the two of them about it. Why didn't they come and get us? I was confused. Janet filled me in that Hobart had told her that being friends of Mr. Stringfellow was assurance we would oblige them in the ongoing investigation. It was a stare down then. I looked at Janet. She looked at me.

On a whim, I picked up the phone and dialed Aunt Jenny again. But I still got an out of order message. The whole situation was getting weirder by the minute. We turned off the machines, got dressed and called a cab. I decided there was no way in hell we were going anywhere in this bizarre town on foot again.

The taxi arrived and we told the cabbie to take us to the morgue. He looked as if he wanted to ask us what was up, but thought better of it. A ten-minute ride to "plug'em and plant'em r-us" cost me fifty bucks and the cabbie had the nerve to ask me if I wanted him to wait. I gave him my "go to hell' look and no tip. He sped off leaving a little rubber and a belch of smoke from the tail pipe.

When we got inside there was a glassed-in counter with the words "City Morgue" in gold written across the top. To the right, were two large grey doors, 'Mor' printed on the left one and 'Gue' printed on the right one. As the entrance door closed behind us, we stood there surrounded by the silence of limbo. I took a deep breath and the medicinal smell of the afterlife filled my lungs and rested heavily on my taste buds. I don't know why, but I taste things sometimes when I breathe, and this stuff was the stuff shit was made of. We walked up to the counter and glimpsed at a person sitting behind a desk. At the window was a small bell. I bent down enough to speak through the opening in the glass and said, "Excuse me." I got no reply. I said it again, louder, and still no reply. I huffed and was going to yell, but Janet reached out, touched my arm, and held her hand to her lips to tell me to be quiet. She reached over to gently touch the bell and immediately the man behind the desk looked up.

"Hello, may I help you?" came from him. Not quite mannish nor womanish, the sound of his voice was like a fast breeze floating past your ears. I shook my head and told him we were there to meet Officer Hobart. His demeanor changed at that comment and he literally jumped from his seat.

"Yes, yes, do come in." His head was going left and right so fast he was stirring a breeze. I guess he was looking for anything that would give him assistance. He took a deep breath finally and said that Hobart was waiting in the coroner's office and he'd ring us in. Just follow the red line painted on the wall and go to Room C. We heard a buzz and a click and the right gray door opened enough to let you know it was unlocked. Janet and I moved into the hallway and did as we were told. We followed the red line painted on the wall and Room C came up pretty fast as the first room on the right when we entered the hall. We stood in that area for a few minutes, then we heard voices coming from the opposite direction. It was Hobart and the coroner. We watched them as they approached and I thought the coroner looked like he probably lived here. He had a pale coloring to him. Hobart gave us his two-finger cap salute. I nodded and Janet smiled.

Hobart introduced us to the coroner who was a Mr. Gruinwa. Upon shaking his hand, I knew for sure he lived in this place. God, his hands felt nasty. If you've ever held a fish that's been out of water for a while, it was something like that. He extended his hand to Janet, but she just nodded to him. There was that pregnant pause that comes along in times like these and then it was over. Hobart spoke up and directed us with a command to view the body.

I spoke up and said, "Wait, you said over the phone you would tell us what the skinny was here." He gave me one of those cop haughty looks and I in turn looked at him with an expression he'd seen when I pummeled him. He started talking then.

"Okay, okay slow down now. We were notified that this John Doe was brought to the morgue sometime last night and just deposited at the door. Mr. Gruinwa here found him sitting up against the front door."

I looked at Gruinwa and he told us of how he came to work that morning to see the deceased sitting up by the front door. Mr. Gruinwa said he thought he was one of the locals who had had too much to drink. He approached the man and touched him on the shoulder and shook him. Mr. Gruinwa turned a little pale then, his voice sounded as though it were shaking as he related what took place next.

"I placed my hand on his shoulder and just shook him a little; not hard, just a little, then his torso fell forward. I stood there transfixed for a moment as his head, shoulders, and arms fell forward and he looked as if he were doing a sit-up. I've been a coroner a long time, but this was 'unreal' as they say. I stepped back and I must have stood there for a while before Mr. Tibido came to work. When he saw me there, he touched me on my arm and I jumped out of my skin. After I'd calmed down a bit, we got a gurney and brought him inside. I then called the police and here we are."

Hobart chimed in then and said he had been informed about the "stiff" and came to look at it. He normally wouldn't have, but the weirdness surrounding the disfigurement of the body, or better yet, the lack of body said he needed to look into this one. I asked him why a detective wasn't assigned to this case. He told me the department was "pushed" at the moment and he was acting in the capacity of detective. He was up for promotion and this was just the thing to get him to the next level; the solving of a murder or in this case, maybe two.

With that remark came a snicker of a smile from Hobart. I let it pass, but put it in the back of my mind with the other reasons I did not like Hobart. For all the bright lights and cleanliness of the morgue, this place could really give you the creeps if you dwelled on it. Janet was visibly shaken and I could tell she wanted to get the hell out of the place. I looked at the two other men and suggested we get this shit done and asked to see the body. Mr. Gruinwa looked at Hobart and Hobart nodded his okay. He then pushed a button on the intercom and told Mr. Tibido to come to Room C. He must have been standing behind the door, because he popped in as soon as Gruinwa's finger left the button.

Tibido hurriedly moved to a gurney in the corner of the room and rolled it to where we were standing. His eyes darted back and forth between the "goon squad" and us. Once the gurney was settled, he put one hand on the sheet that draped the body. Gruinwa nodded and in a dramatic flare he threw back the sheet like he was twirling a cape. It billowed like an albino wave across the lifeless hulk that lay there. A strong medicinal smell sprung from the body. Janet gagged as I stood there in all my manliness holding down my chunks, but turning the proverbial green around the gills. However, I hung. I thought for a moment that these other human beings must have the strongest constitutions in the world or they were so accustomed to this type of degradation, they'd steeled themselves to the intensity of the event.

Janet was tugging at me and I gave her my

handkerchief. Though all her wretching was dry, the motions caused her nose to run and tears to roll. Gruinwa shot a look at Tibido that would have skinned a cat.

"I'm sorry I should have prepared you for what was about to transpire, but Mr. Tibido misunderstood my gesture to him. I wanted him to give you the odor mask to put under your noses and give you some background on the body." I caught Hobart snickering. Tibido's eyes were lit up like a deer's in headlights.

Janet held the handkerchief in front of her face and told us all to shut up and get on with why we were there. Hobart spoke up and said, "You're here because the deceased sort of indicated you folks had had some sort of interaction before he departed this earth."

Janet and I looked at each other. "Hold on now. What makes you think we had anything to do with this?"

Hobart reached in a manila envelope he was carrying and took out a clear plastic bag holding it up for us to see. Inside the bag was what looked to be a small, gold bracelet. Janet took a quick breath and grabbed my arm. My mind threw me back to the night we were looking for Ce. The attempted robbery scene filled the landscape in my head and in a wink I remembered seeing a glint of gold fall to the sidewalk when Janet slid down the wall. Why didn't I see it that night? Damn. Hobart must have seen the recognition in my face. He spoke up and made a crack about the "swamp getting deeper." I shrugged it off. I looked at Janet and her coloring was changing back to normal. The smell wasn't as bad as when we first came in and standing there next to the thing that once was a man wasn't as shocking.

I said, "Okay, what's going on here? Where did you get that bracelet?" Gruinwa spoke this time and responded.

"We found it sewn inside the mouth of this

miscreant. Now, I've studied this sort of hocus pocus because so many here in Louisiana are into this parlor voodoo. Oddly enough, the bracelet was inside a gray bag along with a number of items that, of course if you believe in that nonsense, would, I believe according to my studies, relieve this poor soul of life long hate and suffering and guide him to rest over at the other side of the ethereal plane." Hobart chimed in with, a comment about "Voodoo bullshit" and shook his head in disapproval.

I was listening to these two butt wipes and trying to keep an eye on Janet to make sure she didn't heave. I watched her fumbling in her purse for something. Interrupting Gruinwa, she shouted Ah! Ha! Everyone turned to look at her and she was holding a bracelet in her hand; a bracelet made of 24 carat gold. Hobart unwrapped his hand around the bag that held the "voodoo" bracelet. He held it up and Janet walked quickly over to him and held hers up next to the bagged one. I know I was stunned, and the way it looked, so was everyone else. Hobart motioned us over to one of the unused autopsy tables. Gruinwa, and his shadow, Tibido, were close on his heels.

Hobart laid the bagged bracelet on the table and with a pair of forceps laying there in the array of instruments, he gingerly removed the bracelet and laid it next to the bag. He asked Janet to put her bracelet next to the first one. She complied. They were the same. Each ornately lettered initial stood out next to the other one as if they had been given as twins to the same person.

Damnnnnn! Hobart exclaimed. "What is with you people and evidence?"

"Beats the hell out of me," I said. Hobart then said something about making a phone call. He told us to stay put and he'd be back soon. He headed for the door and swung it open as though he was trying to tear it off its hinges. I immediately started grilling Gruinwa.

"Okay buddy, what's the skinny on the stiff for real? Is it spooked or something? Is there a rational explanation for what happened to the guy?" Gruinwa was taken aback at my forwardness and hesitated to speak. I told him to start flapping his gums or I'd kick his ass into next week. That shook him from his moment and he started to open the floodgates. The body was found as he had stated and after a thorough examination, the bracelet was discovered.

"Yeah, I got all that" I said. "What about that big asshole in the torso?"

He walked over to the body and we followed. He picked up a scalpel, bent over the body, and poked at the tissue where the hole was.

"Look," he said. I leaned down. "I don't know if you have any medical background so I'll say all this in layman's terms. The tissue looks as though it's been bitten, chewed, eviscerated, if you will, and by some sort of wild animal. But, here's the rub." and he hunkered down further and took a small magnifying glass from somewhere. "See, these teeth marks are human as though our friend was also the victim of a human agent." I stood up fast.

"You are shittin' me, man."

" No, no I'm not. I'm being as truthful as possible." I flashed back to that night, the night Janet and I had left this guy alive and the strange sensation I got when Ce went to help Janet. The glint from those teeth of his was difficult to forget. I stood there stone cold for a second, then Hobart slammed his way back into the room.

"Okay, Okay, you can go. I can't hold on anything now. I want to keep your bracelet; the one you brought with you this time." He didn't catch a breath or skip a beat. He looked at Janet and I as though we were going to say no, but Janet held it out to him. She looked at me and I nodded my okay.

"Well, okay. That's all for right now", he said, "but don't leave town and stay off the streets."

"No problem, cappy. We're battened down for the storm." I thought I'd throw some smush at him to irritate the peckerwood. I guess it did; he blew out of the room as he had re-entered a few minutes ago, in a huff and in the wake of the slamming door.

Janet took my arm and we nodded goodbye to our host, then we left, too. Almost.

"Excuse me, don't you want to hear the rest of the material concerning our expired friend?" I looked at Janet and she wanted to go, period. But the way old Gruinwa looked as though he'd be hurt if we just took off, intrigued me. I guess they didn't get many visitors at the morgue that could listen too much and well, what the hell. I patted Janet on the hand and told her just a minute and then we'd go. I motioned to Gruinwa and we headed back to the body.

"As I was saying earlier, a human agent was also involved. Whoever helped the ravenous beast devour the torso of this fellow was unique. I sent a sample of tissue to the lab at the university to see if they could determine the nature of the beast and possibly the identity of the human element. They tested the DNA on the tissue and came up with only one, mind you, one DNA genome." I looked at him with a "what the hell are you talking about" look.

He piped up, "They both have the same DNA; the animal and the man are the same, or the man has no DNA. We know that's not possible; everyone has DNA. So, our protagonist is something that defies science. I, for one, think we are the victims of an extremely brilliant mind; mad, grotesque, dangerous, but none the less, a brilliant mind." He seemed almost admiring of the criminal.

I didn't care at that moment, what or who the perpetrator was. The hairs on the back of my neck were tingling and Janet was turning the color of something that wasn't her normal fairness. I started to back away from the whole mess with Janet in tow.

Gruinwa, for some reason, reached out and touched me on the arm and said, "Are you alright?"

At his touch, I stopped and looked at him hard; hard for touching me and hard for stopping me. While looking at him in the face, I noticed something strange begin to take place. Mr. Gruinwa's face distorted. It scrunched up and he began to drool excessively out of the right side of his mouth and from somewhere inside of him a gasping giggle came to surface. He fell to the floor and began to convulse. I grabbed an ink pen from his shirt pocket and placed it in his mouth pushing down on his tongue to keep him from swallowing it. Janet went to the phone on the desk in the corner of the room. She dialed 911 and told them to come to the morgue a person was having an epileptic fit and had gone into convulsions.

I looked at Tibido and he said in a winy voice that he'd never seen Mr.Gruinwa like this. I said Mr. Gruinwa would be alright and told him not to worry. The paramedics would be here soon. Janet came over to me and said that the 911 operator told her that crank calls were against the law and said she was going to report her. Janet was mad as hell and the bright red color in her face indicated hell wasn't far off. I told Janet that all 911 calls are monitored and the operator must not have paid any attention to where the phone call originated. Until they saw it was a legitimate call, we needed someone.

I reached in my pocket and gave her Hobart's card and told her to call Slick and get his happy ass down here with an ambulance or he'd be interviewing us again about another body. That seemed to set her in motion again and she dialed the phone number. Gruinwa was gasping, giggling, and thrashing around worse than before and it was all I could do to keep him from biting his tongue off.

Tibido was whining more and twisting his hands. I thought he was doing a, "I got to go piss" dance and hollered for him to go. He ran from the room almost into the wall getting to the door. Janet came back and began helping me with Gruinwa. Her color was returning to normal. He hadn't turned blue yet and his eyes hadn't rolled back into his head. His breathing was shallow and gasping. She spoke to him in a calm voice, assuring him help was on the way and he would be alright. He seemed to calm somewhat.

After a minute of this calm, she told me Hobart was coming and bringing paramedics. She said he wasn't too happy hearing from her, but when she told him what had happened, he had commented about "Dammmmm, dumb ass." Janet had asked him who he was calling a dumbass, asshole? He sputtered and spat and assured her he was talking about the 911 service and not her. She told him his apology was accepted and hung up on him.

I thought out loud and said, "That ought to get him running."

We heard sirens within a few seconds and knew Hobart was on the way with the paramedics. Gruinwa was almost sedate about the time the paramedics came busting into the room. They pushed us aside and took over. Hobart trailed a little behind the paramedics and started questioning us as soon as he hit the door. Not a hello or howdy do. As his gums were flapping, I snuck a look at Janet and the impish look I got back let me know that my response to Hobart's questions would be welcome, at least by her. Hobart stood there and finished his tirade of whys and wherefores and then looked at me as if I were going to open the floodgates of information.

What he got was, "Were you talking to me? I wasn't listening very well. I used to be schizoid you know, but I'm alright now." Janet let out a giggle; she loved it when I played people who were so self-assured.

A paramedic walked up to us at that point cutting off any response that Hobart may have ill conceived. He said Gruinwa had had an epileptic seizure from the looks of him and the way he was reacting to the meds they'd given him, it was his first bout with this ailment. They were going to take him to the hospital and get a doctor to check him out just to make sure he would not have another episode.

Then, he added, "Doctors are the worst about taking care of themselves. Dr. Gruinwa would be on one of his own slabs if he didn't take care of this." We all shook our heads in agreement, even Hobart.

The paramedic turned away and I focused on Hobart. He was hot. The veins in eyes and on his forehead were popping out and if we'd stayed, he probably would have been riding with Gruinwa. Janet and I said goodbye and headed out of the room when Hobart shouted for us to stop as we got to the door.

He walked over to us and said in a reserved but angry voice, "DON'T LEAVE TOWN." We smiled.

Stopping at the front desk, I picked up the phone and called for a cab. I'd written down the telephone number of the one that had dropped us off and figured one cab was as good as another. We waited outside in the afternoon heat just so we wouldn't have to smell the inside of the morgue anymore and especially to get away from Hobart, What a putz. The cab pulled up and we climbed into the air-conditioned comfort. I told the driver to take us back to our condo and gave him the address. He said he knew right where it was. We left.

Leaning back in the seat, Janet and I both closed our eyes for a moment. I was thinking about how I could get out of this nut case city without having any warrants served on us for fleeing felon charges. I knew that's what old "deputy dog" would have us charged with if we split. So I leaned back and gave it a halfhearted attempt. Janet on the other hand was sweating like a dog. I thought the cool air from our ride would make her feel better, but I guess not. I asked her if she felt okay and she nodded yes. She was just upset about all the bodies and the information Ce was pushing down our throats. I didn't know what to say, so we sat in silence the rest of the way.

When we reached our condo, I paid the driver. We walked into the building and took the elevator to our floor. The closer we got to the room, I began to hear the phone ring. I looked at Janet and saw a look of "Shit!!!! What now?" come over her face. She let go of my hand and waved me on as a signal to get the damn phone and she'd follow. I bounded to the door and opened it as fast as my fat little fingers would allow me. I left the door open and answered the phone on the seventh ring.

"What?" I said. There was a pause and time slid by enough to let Janet come through, shut the door, and lock it.

"Mr. Madison?" The voice on the phone was familiar, but I was flaky with all the nonsense we'd been through and being pissed off didn't help the person on the other end either. "Mr. Madison, this is Mr. Snid. Please return to the tape as soon as possible. Mr. Ce would like to finish this part of his narrative."

Oh Boy. That really burned my ass. I started with, "Listen to me, you little piece of puny dog, zzzzzzzzzzzzzz." He hung up. I slammed the phone down on the receiver and almost busted it. Janet saw the color rise and asked me who was on the phone, so I tried to tell her through clenched teeth with a balled up fist. The fist, she understood, but what came out of my mouth was anybody's guess.

"Calm down, calm down," Janet said. I stood there and fumed a minute or two and then what Janet had intoned set in and I began to breath deeper. Finally, I let the anger go. My fist un-balled and the color drained from my face and I calmed down. It was always a challenge to stay cool.

"Okay sweetie, who was on the phone?" Janet asked again. I spoke coherently this time and told her it was Snid and Ce wanted us back on the couch now. We both held each other for a long minute and headed to the viewing room. I plopped my big ass down and Janet detoured to the kitchen. She brought back some cold drinks. When she handed me the drink, I sucked it down in nothing flat and asked for more. She said okay, she'd get the bottle and bring it to the couch, but there wasn't anything to eat.

Waiting for her to come back from the kitchen, I set both machines on pause so when she returned, I could push START and rejoin our roles as the "captive audience." She didn't return quickly, but as soon as I saw her turn the corner I hit PLAY.

"Whoa boy, settle down, chill. At least let me get my paper and pen to write this material down."

I automatically hit STOP on the remotes at that comment. She put down my drink and hers. She picked up her pen and the legal pad and then she nodded to me.

"Stop," she said. I hit the buttons again. "Just to let you know, I called for pizza again. They said we owed them for two, but I explained about the medical emergency in my special sweet voice and the guy at the pizza place said he'd let the first one slide." I told her she was a good girl, a sweetie.

"Ready?" With a nod from her I hit PLAY again, and both tapes rolled. After a few seconds of snow, we were back in the world of Ceophulus T. Stringfellow.

"I am sorry for that interruption David and I assure you that Officer Hobart will not have cause to bother you and your wife again. Death, at times, can be a tedious thing, then other times it can be organized and

efficient. Oh, how I do carry on."

With that little bit of sharing, the hairs on the nape of my neck rose and stood out like quills on a porcupine. I flashed Janet a look and she was inching closer to me along the couch. I patted the place next to me and she did not hesitate to occupy the spot. Ce looked as though he was looking at us and that also unnerved me.

He gave a faint smile and said, "Children, don't be afraid of Ce. Ce only hunts the monsters." He went on and put his head back like he had done before he went into his earlier narratives. The buzzing of the tape during this momentary lull was deafening. Then he began.

Chapter Nine

Bad Eye was not Dick's only friend, but his closest. There were other kids Dick knew from school and he liked most of them, one in particular, an old boy name "Red". They had run into each other from time to time and talked about hunting and fishing when they did. As I mentioned previously, school was starting soon and Dick knew he would have to go. He tried to quit once and the truant officer came to the house. Dick's father had cussed the man out. His father busted his ass and gave him a black eye for that episode. He also went to school to keep his mother happy. She always told him the smarter he was, the more money he could make for her. This year he would be considered one of the "older boys" and that suited him fine. He had it planned, school and all. He'd go to school in the mornings, check his traps in the afternoons three days a week, set his limb lines on Tuesdays and Thursdays, and divide the weekends up between them. He'd quit fishing when the rains came and concentrate on his traps and hunting. Good plan.

What Dick didn't realize was that along with getting older, his hormones were kicking in and nature had plans, too. Indian summer changed into fall and the harvesting was done. Dick had spent the majority of that time in his haven. When he had money from his efforts, he'd stock the "hole" with can goods and non-perishables. The rest he had given to his mother as promised. On one of his visits, she reminded him that school was starting soon and made him promise that he would go as much as he could as long as it didn't interfere with him bringing her money. Dick loved those options, "as long as it didn't interfere with him bringing her money." That meant he'd have to skip a day here and there in order to maintain his traps and get in the necessary hunting to fill the orders from the storekeeper,

Mr. Barton. It might be a good school year after all.

The first day of school came and Dick showed up late. Traps and limb lines wait for no man. As he entered the classroom, Dick took the look Ms. Pardue, the schoolteacher, threw at him with a grain of salt. He maneuvered himself between the desks to the back of the room. On his way, he saw old faces he knew, but also he looked for faces that weren't there for a second or so, like Bad Eye's. Then he saw a new face.

There were no bells or whistles, angelic choirs, or any of the nonsense associated with the rapture of love at first sight. What caught him off guard was her face; a face as fresh as the first rays of morning sun and eyes that out sparkled any star he'd seen in the sky. She was looking straight at him, and the way the sunlight came streaming through the classroom windows and enveloped her, presented to him a picture of human beauty his rustic life had not prepared him for.

"Dick! Sit down." Ms. Pardue, the teacher, said loudly. The class giggled and Dick moved on, turning his head as he sat to look at her one more time. She was looking at him and smiled. Dick turned redder than a dick on a dog. He quickly dropped his head to stare at the desk top and held as still as he possibly could, just like he was trailing a white tail buck. Now Dick had managed to sit down next to Red, and Red picked up on Dick's consternation. For some reason this just set ol' Red's mind into "let's razz old Dick today." Red smiled a broad smile to himself and set the wheels of good-natured ribbing in motion. He turned to Dick and made smooching sounds. This made Dick flush of course and also made him look toward *her*.

Ms. Pardue finished calling the role, the part of the process Dick interrupted when he came in. She finished with "and Dick Madison, late as usual." She closed her roll book and slapped a ruler down onto the desk so everyone settled down.

"Now class, I want to introduce you all to your new classmate, Annette Toland. Annette, please stand up and tell the class a little about yourself." The petite girl didn't hesitate to stand. When she got up from her seat, she smoothed herself almost like a cat or so Dick thought.

She began with "Hello, my name is Annette Toland and we are from Memphis, Tennessee. My daddy is a lawyer and we've moved here until our new house in Nashville can be completed." She sat down immediately after that statement.

Ms. Pardue thanked her and welcomed her to the class. Dick sat mesmerized. Red, on the other hand, took the opportunity to "accidentally" slam a book to the floor and the report made Dick jump from his seat. He swung around to confront Red, but as luck would have it, the class all had turned toward the commotion.

Ms. Pardue, intoned, "Do you wish to add something, Dick?" Dick turned slowly toward Ms. Pardue and caught the eyes of everyone in the class on him.

Reluctantly he spoke and said, "Uhhhhh. No'm."

"Then sit down," Ms. Pardue barked. This of course evoked a loud laugh from the class. Ol' Dick turned a lot of colors that day. During the course of the morning, Red would plague Dick with catcalls and gestures that would set Dick's fire to rise. During recess Red managed to stay clear of Dick and made it to lunch without being forced to regret his taunts. Now, this isn't to say Dick wasn't going to get Red back, oh no. Dick was formulating a plan, something that would make Red literally see red, and possibly make Ms. Toland see that he was clever.

All through the day Dick would sneak looks at this "China fine" girl from Memphis. Something about his insides stirred him. This stirring was causing him some embarrassment, too. His manhood took upon itself to express a desire to see what was beyond the confines of his overalls. As folks today say, *boner, big time.*

Dick was able to quell these feelings for most of the day, but unfortunately for him in the afternoon reading session, he was called upon to read aloud. This required standing and holding one's book up in front of the face, then reading the passages designated by Ms. Pardue to the whole class. Ms. Pardue might have known Dick was in a state of "natural agitation" and called upon him out of spite. At least he thought that later.

When his name was called to recite, Dick hesitated a minute before standing, trying to put, "things in order." When he did stand, he kept the book down as though he was having a hard time seeing the page and had to read the material from a distance. Ms. Pardue saw through this rouse and told Dick she would have none of that.

"Hold your book up, Dick, and read the first paragraph on page 22." Dick began to read the quote from the textbook. He had a dry throat, stopping and starting a couple of times in between swallows trying to lubricate his vocal cords.

Ms. Pardue cleared her throat loudly and Dick blurted out, "Let us not, be unmindful that, liberty is power, that the nation, blessed, with the largest, portion of liberty, must in proportion to its numbers, be the most powerful nation upon earth. By John Adams."

Dick stood there as blushed and flustered as anyone in his situation would be. Ms. Pardue was looking to the ceiling for a mispronounced word or any stammer or stutter that would have given her cause to humiliate Dick. None occurred.

"Alright Madison, sit down." Dick flopped down into his seat as fast as he could. But the reading was long enough that Red took the opportunity to zing Dick again.

Red blurted out with, "Dick's largest portion is at liberty if you ask me." The whole class roared. Red knew he'd be in trouble for that one and was prepared to go home for the rest of the day. Ms. Pardue rapped her desk with her ruler more than once to quiet the class and when she did that, everyone knew the rest of the day would be soured. Finally, silence drew heavy on the class and Ms. Pardue stood fuming at the front of the room.

Suddenly, she rushed toward Dick and grabbed him by the straps of his overalls. When he came up from his seat, his manhood sprung from the front of his overalls and stood at attention.

Ms. Pardue looked at him and then screamed, "Get out of my class, you filthy boy, and take that red headed no-good with you. I'm going to tell your mother and find out what type of hedonist she's raising. Don't come back to this class until you've learned how to control yourself around decent people." She pushed Dick toward the front door to the classroom. On the way, she grabbed at Red and looked like she was going to box his ears.

Red sat there whining, "What did I do?"

Ms. Pardue looked at him and said, "Go home and wash that filthy mouth of yours out and don't think I'm not going to have your mother find out why you pal around with the likes of that Madison boy. His father's a drunk and his mother is a shameless hussy."

Dick heard this tirade. His embarrassment died faster than it had appeared. The "rage" swelled up inside him, and he wasn't prepared for it. The next thing he felt was the weight of his classmates holding him down and the smell of different body odors pushing into his nostrils. He was barely able to squeak out a, "get off me." Slowly and deliberately, the boys peeled off him one at a time. When he did get up, he quickly surveyed the room. Two of the windows were broken out and Ms. Pardue's desk was

overturned with her belongings strewn all over the floor.
All the girls were huddled around Ms. Pardue. She was
holding her ruler or what was left of it out like a sword
mumbling something about the devil and an inhuman child.
Dick looked for Red. Red was standing by the door wide
eyed. Dick ran toward the door and Red almost fell
backward trying to get out of his way. Dick hollered as he
passed Red, "Come on!"

Red picked up the pace next to Dick as he ran from
the school. Dick looked at Red and asked him what
happened in the classroom. Red explained that Ms. Pardue
had badmouthed his mama and he had gone crazy. He
picked up a couple of chairs and threw them through the
windows and then he picked up the desk and flipped it
over. Then, he just stood there, breathing heavy with
slobber and foam drooling out of his mouth. All the girls
ran to Ms. Pardue and surrounded her while the bigger boys
had tackled him. They laid on him for almost ten minutes
before he calmed down.

Red also told Dick that a couple of the bigger boys
got a few licks in while he was down, that's why his nose
was bleeding. Dick raised his arm to wipe his nose and a
streak of blood showed on his arm. He grunted and began
to slow down now and that was okay with Red because he
was just about done in running. Dick asked Red if the new
girl was hurt at all.

Red laughed at that and said, "Boy, you ain't right.
You no more have a chance with her than the man in the
moon. Her daddy's a lawyer and your daddy's a drunk.
You wear the same clothes every day and no shoes, and
you stink! Do you honestly think that girl or any other girl
would have you on a bet?" Red laughed again and shook
his head.

Dick took all this with a grain of salt and then
suddenly, he pushed Red down to the ground. He stared at

Red and Red saw the anger in Dick's eyes as he pissed on himself. Dick clenched his fist. Red closed his eyes waiting for the pounding Dick was about to give him.

It never came. Red lay there a minute longer and then he opened one eye and to his astonishment there was no Dick. Red sat up and looked all around him. Nothing but the noise of the woods surrounded him; the dirt road he was sitting on was a dustless wasteland. He was alone. He shrugged his shoulders and let out with a, "Damnnnn." Red picked himself up and started toward home dusting himself off as much as possible. He stunk from urine mixed with the dust from the road; the wet stain stood out.

He knew when he got home he'd be in trouble. By now, Ms. Pardue would have surely gotten in touch with his mother. She'd meet him at the front door and stare a hole through him for a minute or two. Her first words to him would be to clean himself up. After he cleaned up, she would make him go plow in the bottom until dark when his father would be home. When he got back to the house after putting up the mule and plow, his father would wear his ass out and he'd not be able to walk right for days. That thought and what Dick might have in store for him kept him jumpy all the way home.

Dick had been standing over Red with the intention of beating the tar out of him. When he saw Red piss on himself, the feeling of revenge was good, but that's all, just good. Red still had to pay for the taunts and the brutal truth he'd thrust at Dick about not having a chance with the girl and his lack of proper clothes and all. This wretched feeling overflowed in Dick and a plan of total revenge filled his head. He looked at Red lying on the dirt road and then he took to the woods toward the "hole" and his 4-10.

Dick figured he'd get his shotgun and circumvent the long way to Red's place by using the woods as a short cut. He snaked in and out of the "hole" with the 4-10 and one shell. One shell was all he'd need. He'd pepper Red's ass with enough shot that he'd always remember that Dick Madison was not dirt and to mess with him was to mess with hell itself. Or so Dick's mind convinced itself. It was moving in and out of the "rage" so fast, the thought process was muddled. The rage made him think that the pain he inflicted on someone was greater than the pain they inflicted on him, and eventually the pain he felt would turn into strength. He held to a belief that "Might, makes right."

At that moment Dick was as right as rain. He slunk through the woods like a wild thing. Cautious, alert, single minded, the anger focused Dick and moved him surrealistically to a sight for an ambush. Red was at the other end of the field when Dick saw him through the underbrush at the edge of the wood. Red's plowing pattern would make him swing at the end of the field where Dick was and turn to furrow. Red's father liked his fields tilled east to west after the harvest. It was some old farmers' superstition about the way the winter sun warmed the earth just enough to let the tired earth sleep in comfort or something like that.

Red plodded along behind the mule, Roscoe, who knew his job better than most and Red's job was just to guide the plow. If you have to "run" a mule in the field you'd *gee* and *haw* your way around that patch of ground. That was a waste of mule and daylight. Roscoe began to make the wide arch at the end of the field and exposed Red's backside. Dick had positioned himself to get a clear shot at his antagonist. During the few seconds Red would stand still as Roscoe moved to face west, was when Dick would open fire.

Bang. The retort from Dick's 4-10 sounded like a lost thunder clap the way it resonated through the field and bounced off the tree lined edges. Dick saw Red jump from the pellets that slammed into his ass. He screamed like a girl and fell to the ground. Dick could still hear Red hollering as he took off. The anger that drove him to shoot Red suddenly went away and left him totally alone with what he'd done. That's one of the bad after effects of the "rage." After it makes you lash out at the pain, it leaves you as fast as a fart in a hurricane. His first inclination was to help Red, but his body seemed to push him to run.

Dick ran to the "hole" and hid the 4-10. He then scampered to his house and hid under the back porch like he did sometimes when the old man was raving. Dick pushed himself against the foundation to the point he felt he was going to become part of the stone. Lying there, his mind made him think of Red, and when he did, bile filled his gut and backed up into his mouth leaving a nasty taste. Dick made himself think of other things. He was certain no one knew where the hole was. Bad Eye and he had a pact and he knew Bad Eye would not have told anyone and he knew he hadn't.

Dick heard his momma come in the front door. She was talking to someone. It was the sheriff. Dick had a run in with him before and never forgot that voice. The sheriff was telling Bessie that he'd gotten a call from a hysterical woman who said her son had been shot in the *behind* by Dick. He asked Bessie if she'd seen Dick. There was a moment of dead air, then Bessie told the sheriff, "Dick stays away from here most of the time, Sheriff. His father and he don't get along."

"Do you know where he is, Mrs. Madison?"

"No sheriff, I don't. He stays in the woods by the river when he's not here." The sheriff asked her a lot of questions about Dick, all of which she answered truthfully. Bessie asked about the boy Dick was to have shot, and the sheriff told her that he was at the local hospital recuperating and he'd be alright in a day or so.

"He'd be alright, that is, if his folks pressed charges.

Your boy is either lucky he didn't do permanent damage to the other child or a damn good shot. By the way, while I'm here, where does your husband keep his guns?" Bessie thought for a moment and told him he kept them locked up in the bedroom in his closet. "You mind if I take a look at them, Ms. Bessie?" Dick's mama didn't say anything.

Dick heard footsteps, two distinct sets, move to the part of the house where Dick's parents had their bedroom. The sheriff asked Bessie to open the closet, but she said Dick's father had the only key and he was over in Humphreys County moving logs today. Dick heard the hard footfalls of the sheriff's boots as he moved to the closet door. He wondered if the sheriff was really just a snoop.

"Looks like your boy didn't get the gun from here. It would take more than an eleven year old to pop this hardware. Is there a friend or an acquaintance Dick may have gotten a gun from, Ms. Bessie?"

"I don't know sheriff... unless, he got it from down in the root cellar." The footfalls were fast and the creaking hinge on the root cellar door let Dick know that he was soon to be found out at last about having the 4-10.

Dick waited a few minutes listening to the two adults mill around in the root cellar when he decided that bravado might be the course of the day. Besides, he was hungry. He crawled out from under the porch and dusted himself off as best he could. He walked up the back steps and opened the screen, then the back door. The backdoor stuck tight in one place and normally when it was opened, the door would hang and open with a loud popping sound. Dick had learned long ago how to steadily push the door toward the hinges and it would open as if it were brand new and not make any noise at all. He stood inside the kitchen and the movement down in the cellar was muffled now. He slid across the floor like a snowflake over frozen water, opened the breadbox pulling out a loaf of bread. He normally used his homemade knife to cut things, but today he thought he'd just use his mamma's knife in the drawer. He sliced himself a big hunk of bread and lifted the cloth off the covered pork steak on the counter. He placed a piece of the meat on the bread and began eating the open face sandwich. He opened the icebox, poured himself a glass of cold milk, and pulled a chair out from the kitchen table. Dick let the heavy chair scratch across floor and set next to the trap door leading down to the cellar and waited. He heard all the commotion from the cellar stop. Then he heard a rush of footsteps to the ladder. Up popped the sheriff's head like a groundhog looking for a clear day.

"Boy, don't move," came from the sheriff's mouth as he saw Dick just sitting there eating. The sheriff pulled himself out of the opening somewhat ungraciously. Bessie hesitated for a minute, then she came up from the cellar. She closed the cellar door and swung around to Dick.

"Honey, what have you done, what have you done?" Dick was just about to say something when the sheriff backhanded Dick out of the chair. The milk and sandwich flew across the room as Dick fell to his knees. A stream of bright red blood flowed from Dick's nose. Bessie started crying and wringing her hands the way she did when Dick's father slapped him around. Dick looked up, but sheriff didn't see Dick's eyes and how they were filling up with hate; red, raging, hate.

The sheriff lifted Dick up off the kitchen floor with a kick to his belly. Dick rolled like a bass trying to throw a plug and landed flat, face down on the floor. This time he just lay there. Bessie stood there frightened; so frightened she probably would have let the sheriff kill Dick and never said a thing but, the sheriff wasn't about to try and explain the beating death of a child. With grown men, it wasn't too hard to explain away an "accidental" beating to anyone who investigated.

He picked Dick up off the floor by the straps of his overalls and slapped him down in the chair again. The sheriff looked at Bessie and told her to clean Dick up. She took a dishrag, wet it, and wiped Dick's mouth and nose. She pushed against his stomach and Dick flinched. After Bessie cleaned Dick up, the sheriff walked over to him, grabbed his face, and gave it a quick left to right look.

He said out loud, "He's okay. Now get up, boy." Dick stood up as a pain-filled grunt passed his lips and he doubled over. When he had righted himself, Bessie tried to hug him, but Dick pulled away. He quickly gave her a kiss and started toward the front door. He knew if he had allowed her to hold him, he would have let the pain and his childishness break him down. He knew he had to be strong. This sheriff, this "John Law," was known for his brutality to all comers; man, woman, or child. He walked behind Dick and pushed him to make him go faster.

Bessie began to cry again and sank down in the chair Dick had occupied. The thought struck her that if Dick was taken away, she would have to scrape up the money herself for the new hat she wanted from the Sears and Roebuck catalog. Then, her thoughts went to what she was going to say to Dick's father when he came back from his trip. "Oh poor, poor me," she said out loud. "Poor me."

Chapter Ten

Dick walked up to the sheriff's old truck. He kept his back to the lawman who would give Dick a kick or another push if he gave him half a chance.

"Get in, sit down, and keep your mouth shut." The sheriff walked around to the driver's side of the truck, adjusted his pants and utility belt, then stuck a finger in his mouth. He removed a big wad of tobacco and let it fall to the ground. Reaching in the truck, he pulled a small mason jar from the backside of the seat and opening it, took a pull of the clear liquid. Dick knew it was "potato peel'ins" as some of the ol' boys called it. Moonshine was part of the world in those days. The sheriff got into the truck, placed the mason jar between his legs, and started up the motor. He put the gears to DRIVE and headed out of the graveled drive onto the dirt road. Dick didn't look back; he knew his mother wouldn't be there.

The sheriff tried to coax Dick into telling him where the shotgun was hidden, but Dick just sat there looking out the window watching the landscape roll by at the breakneck speed of 15 miles an hour. The sheriff punched Dick a couple of times in order to make him talk, but Dick just hunkered down in the seat closer to the door. Agitated because he might be late for his supper at the boarding house, the sheriff was extra mean out of hunger. Taking Dick by the jail house and then getting to Ms. Judith's house would make him have to rush and he was not a "rushing" type of person.

"Boy, if you make me late for supper, I'll cut your balls off and feed them to the dogs." Dick half heard the sheriff's ramblings, but his mind was rolling to and from the events of the day and the possible outcome of what he had done. At one point, he saw himself on a chain gang working in the road in front of his mamma's house, and his father was the guard overseeing the men. His father held a razor strap and was brandishing it above his head as if he were going to strike Dick.

"Boy? Are you listnun' to me, boy?" Dick blurted out a terse no. The sheriff grabbed him by the top of his head, pulling his hair which made Dick come out of his hunkered position to sit high on the seat. Dick saw the jailhouse in front of him now and instinctively he shuddered.

The rumors about this place ran piecemeal through his mind. There was the one about old man Matson that stuck out strongly in his mind. Seems Mr. Matson had gotten "drunked" up and made the mistake of talking to the mayor's wife about "unseemly" matters concerning her weight. From what had been passed around, Matson told her that when she walked, her ass looked like two suckl'in pigs in a tote sack fighting each other. She took offense at that and the mayor had Matson hauled in for being drunk in public. Seems when he came out of the jailhouse, he couldn't talk anymore. The sheriff had cut out his tongue. Of course, and as a matter of record, the "prisoner had a seizure and bit his tongue off before help arrived. The cause of the seizure was the DT's."

The sheriff cut off the engine of the truck and almost jumped out of the seat. He told Dick to get out, but Dick sat where he was. The sheriff reached through the window and punched Dick hard enough to make him woozy, but not hard enough to knock him out. Then opening the door, he drug Dick out of the truck. Hanging on to Dick's suspenders, he pulled the young angry boy along the broken stone walkway like he was carrying a sack of potatoes. The door of the jailhouse opened and the stench of old cigars, urine, and human corruption assailed Dick's nostrils. It was as if the sheriff had pushed an ammonia capsule under Dick's nose.

Having never seen the inside of the jailhouse, the boy's instinct surveyed the office as best and as fast as he could. Old wanted circulars, campaign posters, peeling paint, and down right filth greeted his abrupt awareness. The two cells in the back of the jailhouse were made with old flat iron bars. Above the cell on the left was an aged sign that said, "Whites." On the right was an aged sign that said, "Negroes."

Dick made the mistake of pulling back at the door. The sheriff coming from behind, kicked Dick and literally lifted him off the floor and propelled him into the open area of the jailhouse. With his hands cuffed behind him, he hit the floor with his right shoulder and the right side of his face taking most of the fall. The sheriff walked over to his ramshackled desk and fumbled for the keys that unlocked the cells. A many keys that were on the ring, he had access to anything and everything else he needed to open in the his filthy, sick world.

Dick had worked himself into a cockeyed sitting position where he had landed. The sheriff looked at him and as if he were talking to someone else, he asked, "What am I going to do with you, boy?" He stared at the disheveled lump of misery on the floor and as he stood there, an idea popped into his head. Out loud he blared, "Fuck yeah."

He moved with the speed that fat people used when they get hungry, fast and furious. He headed toward a door in the back of the room. Dick watched him as he opened it with one of his keys and a shudder ran down Dick's spine. The first thought that came to Dick was the sheriff putting him in that room and locking him in it. As the door swung open, stuff fell out onto the floor. Dick slid a little along the floor to get a better look at what the sheriff was doing and saw that the room was a junk room, small and jammed with all kinds of crap. The sheriff tore through the mess and finally came out with a harness and shackles.

Turning to Dick he said, "Get up, boy. Come over here." Dick watched the sheriff walk over to a large iron ring that protruded out of the floor near the cells. It was far enough away so no contact could be made if anyone occupied the cell nearest the ring. Dick struggled to his feet and hobbled over to where the sheriff waited.

"Stand here, boy, and stand still. If you make me late for my supper, you'll eat your own shit before you'll get a meal from me." Dick stood as still as the pain would let him. The sheriff unlocked the cuffs and Dick's sore arms fell free. The sheriff then told Dick to spread his legs and hold his arms up in the air. The wrenching pain Dick felt when he raised his arms almost made him scream, but he held it in. The sheriff slapped the manacles around Dick's ankles, hooked the getup to a belt harness, then he put wrist restraints around Dick's wrists and hooked them to the harness. All this was then laced with a log chain and locked to the ring coming out of the floor.

"This is what they used to do to runaways, boy. Ain't you lucky?" Dick fell to his knees. The hot liquid that tears are made from when a person is angry pushed out of Dick's eyes. He tried to hold them back, but this time…this time his resolve failed him. The sheriff let out a snicker and "I knew I'd break you."

The cruel fat man tossed the keys back to the desk and moved to the door. "If I think about it, I'll bring you back a bone or two. You'll make a good dog, boy, a good dog by the time I'm through with you." Finally he left the jailhouse to go stuff his gut. Dick still sat with his knees on the floor. A deep, horrible, crushing feeling pushed on his soul. He knew he would die, soon. Being cooped up and tied like a dog would surely kill him. The tears welled up in his eyes again and thoughts of not seeing his momma almost choked him. He sat there in his self-pity and blubbered. But there was something in Dick's makeup; something that transcended his desperation and swept his pity away like you'd sweep the dirt off a sidewalk. Anger, revenge, hate; call it what you will, it took Dick back to the situation at hand. *It all pushed him one step closer to being a man before his time.*

The sound of the truck starting brought Dick's head up. He listened attentively to the sound of it pulling away from the building. He waited and counted in his head, "one thousand one, one thousand two," and on. When he got to one thousand one hundred twenty, he pushed himself up from the floor. He put his feet together and stood directly over the ring. He bent over and began to push the shackles down over the legs of his overalls. The shackles touched skin and after a few minutes, the pants legs were out of the shackles. Dick stood on his tiptoes and began to work the shackle over his left foot. It took him a few hard pushes, but he got it done. He then worked on the right foot and got that one free, too. Having freed his legs, he could stand and bend even though he was still tethered to the ring in the floor. The sheriff should have spent more time securing his catch and let his stomach cool its heels.

Dick reached down into the ruler pocket of his overalls and pulled out his homemade knife. Honing the blade on sand stone once or twice a week kept the blade sharp, sharp enough to cut through the old heavy leather wrist restraints that were the last hurdle keeping Dick from his goal of being free. The bonds fell to the floor as Dick made short work of the leather. He slid the knife back into its hiding place. Taking a deep breath to fill his heaving lungs, Dick coughed and spat a hocker on the ring that had been used to hold too many men, right or wrong.

Dick could have run, but he had nowhere to go except the "hole." He knew if he did that, sooner or later the sheriff would get Mr. Grabber and his bloodhounds and they'd find him. They could find anything if they got the scent. He'd seen these animals running deer near the river and they stopped dead in their tracks when they picked up a buck's spore where he'd pissed on a deadfall. Usually a deer ran like hell and tried to swim the river. Dick knew if the dogs got the deer in the water they'd badger it until it drowned. After they killed it, they always swam back to shore and let the current sweep the deer down river letting the carcass rot. The dogs would then go and find something else to terrorize.

One particular time though, Dick had been nearby and was sickened by the whole ritual. His scent pulled the dogs away from the deer and it escaped ill fate. When they started trailing Dick, he screwed their hunt by putting cayenne pepper in a clearing and pissing all around the area. They didn't know whether to shit or go blind. With a nose full of cayenne, those dogs couldn't hunt for a week. Dick knew they'd remember his spore and being dumb brutes, they'd be angrier at him than scared of the cayenne.

He walked over to the sheriff's desk and pulled the big leather chair out, flopping down into it. If someone were watching him, he would have looked just like a child playing, but Dick's mind was concocting a plan. Dick started opening the desk drawers. He found a bunch of wanted posters, pads, pencils, and everyday crap. In one drawer he found some cigars and a flask. He opened the flask and smelled the whiskey. He turned up his nose to the strong odor, left the cap off, dropped it back inside, and then shut the drawer. There was another drawer that had old hand guns in it, but after a quick look, he saw they were all unloaded or busted. He slammed that one shut and opened the last one that contained a bunch of knives. Some were rusted, old hunting knives, or folding knives and some were broken. He quickly eyed the disgusting , filthy junk. Dick fumbled through the bunch and was going to close that drawer, when out of the corner of his eye he spotted a pearl handled beauty, an "Arkansas toothpick" as it was called for good reason. Now you know, a "toothpick" was normally carried by a gambler or a cultured man. When Jim Bowie had his, it was named after him, the Bowie Knife. The sheriff must have taken it off some good ol' boy, or it was a leftover from some poor bastard who made the mistake of running into the sheriff.

Dick held the blade by its pearl handle and eyed the dangerous blade with questioning enthusiasm. It seemed sturdy enough, but Dick wondered if it could handle the riggers of everyday use. He reached into the pocket of his overalls that held his homemade skinner and put it in his left hand with the "toothpick" in his right. He weighted the heft of each blade and then he stood up and walked to the center of the room.

The young expert fingered each knife until his practiced hands found the balance of each blade. He looked at the wall that had most of the wanted posters on it. Spying the most vicious criminal, Dick took a stance that allowed his feet to be firm on the floor and in direct confrontation with the poster. He lowered his arms to his sides and took a deep breath. He exhaled, and as he did, his arms came up in unison. The air was split by the almost inaudible sound of two blades being let loose at the same time. The resounding thud was so in sync; one would have sworn the blades had hit at the same time. Dick walk-ran to the wall and viewed his precision throw. The villain's nose on the poster was cut in two by this marksman's tools. Dick pulled the knives from the wall in an up and down sawing motion and each one came smoothly from its perch. He mentally marked the depth of penetration on each one and knew that at the strength he'd thrown them, the villain would have, if the situation were real, met his maker breathing out his armpits because his nose would no longer be part of his face. A broad smile quickly came to his. He knew what he would do when the sheriff came back from supper.

Dick didn't know that part of the sheriff's routine was to sit on the front porch with the other tenants of the boarding house. After supper, they would belch, pass gas, and tell tall tales of manly exploits that were based on fantasy more than fact. So, he watched the old clock on the wall behind the sheriff's desk. Its tick tock melody became hypnotic, the swift movement of the minute hand adding to the monotony.

As he watched and listened, he nodded off a time or two, then finally fell into a light, but fitful sleep. His fits were caused by the sight of his mother crying, begging him to come back to her, then her question, *"Who's going to give me money to buy my new hat?"* Then, the scene changed to the sheriff kicking him and slapping him in the face. As the sheriff's foot came close to his stomach, he saw his father's face outlined in the sheriff's, and then he felt the pain of the blow again.

He awoke sweating and made himself move. He first crouched, then pushed himself up and away from the desk where he'd been sleeping. He looked at the tormenting clock and saw that almost two hours had passed since the sheriff had gone and Dick began to wonder if the sheriff was ever coming back. The quiet and concern were squelched soon enough. Dick picked up on the noise the engine of the sheriff's truck made and knew the sheriff would be coming through the door soon.

The engine noise grew louder and Dick prepared himself. When he heard the door of the truck slam, he raced back to the tethers and restraints he'd cut. He placed the anklets back around his legs and sat on the floor with the hope the sheriff wouldn't see anything wrong until Dick did it for him. The wrist restraints were harder to control, but Dick managed by putting them on his thighs, close to his stomach, and hiding the cuts to the leather with his body. He sat on the floor with his head bowed and waited. The sheriff opened the door to the jailhouse. He saw Dick sitting on the floor by the ring. Dick's head was bowed and he looked as if he were asleep. The sheriff had a plate in his hand covered by an old dishrag. The plate held some meat scraps and the hard end of a piece of cornbread. The sheriff hung his hat on the old coat rack by the front door, then hollered for Dick to wake up.

"Boy, get your ass up and get this supper I brung you." Dick didn't move. He was seething and frightened, hoping his charade was working on the dumbass. The sheriff walked over to Dick and looked him over a second, then kicked at him. Dick stirred a little. The sheriff backed off when Dick slowly looked up at him with a whipped hound look. Then, he responded with "Boy, you alright, you sick?" Dick lowered his head back down to rest on his chest. The sheriff walked back up to Dick and leaned down, down into Dick's rage.

Dick's hands moved with practiced speed and the sheriff found himself being held by the shirt collar with something pricking his neck. The little pinprick made the sheriff start to sweat and his bulging eyes picked up on the red drops of blood falling onto the dishrag that covered the food on the plate still in his hand. Dick jumped up from his sitting position knocking the plate from the sheriff's hand. The sheriff instinctively reached for his holster and sidearm. The blade on the "toothpick" went deeper into his throat and he stopped his hand in mid-stride.

Still holding onto the sheriff's collar, Dick pushed the big man against the wall. He reached and unholstered the sheriff's gun. Pulling the long neck colt from its rest, Dick pushed the button on the weapon's side that dislodged the cylinder from the hammer and barrel. Shaking the gun until all the shells fell to the floor, he kicked them away and threw the gun across the room. Dick pushed the sheriff to make him move and herded him toward the storage closet where the sheriff had pulled out the restraints for Dick. He knew there had to be more of those things in there. If not, he'd have to come up with some rope to do the job. His mind raced with a plan for freedom and revenge.

Holding the knife to the sheriff's throat hard enough to make the sheriff look at the ceiling, Dick quickly surveyed the closet and saw a set of leggings. He grabbed them and pushed the sheriff back to the ring, dropped them, and coldly told the sheriff to put them on. The sheriff began to get the leggings and as he bent over, Dick adjusted the blade to slice open the sheriff's already bloody throat if it became necessary. The sheriff put on one of the leggings and locked it. Dick made him pull the other one through the ring so the chain lay inside the ring. He hurried the sheriff with a well-placed bit of pressure on the knife.

The sheriff suddenly stood straight up and tried to knock Dick over, but Dick sidestepped him and swung the blade to arc. The strong thin point cut through the sheriff's cheek. The big jerk screamed a little girl scream and grabbed at his face with his hands. Dick took the keys and cuffs from the sheriff and pulled his arms behind him snapping the cuffs on him. The not-so-mighty sheriff stood there and looked at Dick with cowardess and fear. Dick came up to the big man and kicked him behind the right knee and the fat man fell backwards knocking his head on the floor. The old wood of the floor made the sheriff's scull sound like it was hollow.

Dick went to the water bucket and fetched a gourd full of the liquid. He stood over the lump of flesh flopped on the floor and doused the fat face with the water. The sheriff sputtered back to life and shook his head to clear away the cobwebs from the fall. He realized he couldn't move his hands and his feet were hobbled. Dick stood off for a minute or two to let the ol' boy get his wits about him. The Sheriff blubbered, "Dick, don't do this, it will be easier on you if you don't. Let me go and we'll forget all about this." The bruised young boy looked at his quarry and turned the "toothpick" over in his hand, then he ran his left hand through his hair. A long second walked its way across the silence. Dick lay flat down on the floor and inched his way to the sheriff.

He put his lips up to the sheriff's right ear and said in a cold, hard voice, "Don't come looking for me. Red's not dead. My momma needs me. I'm all she's got." The sheriff started in with a tirade about his father, and how Dick was going to get the beating of his life when he got home. Dick positioned his face close to the sheriff's so the sheriff could get a good look at him. Then, he steeled his eyes and brought the "toothpick" up to the sheriff's nose.

The flesh Dick cut made a sound of "flick, flick," when Dick sliced through it. The sheriff screamed and pissed himself. Dick had cut the sheriff's nostrils and blood was flowing into the sheriff's mouth. The old fart started crying, cussing, making threats, sobbing, and finally pleading with Dick not to cut him any more.

Dick edged up to the sheriff's right ear again to say, "I'm leaving now. Don't follow me, and don't bother my momma again." Dick didn't make any threats, he just told it like it was. His folks didn't have a telephone, so by the time Dick got around to getting home, it would be tomorrow. He didn't care if his father heard about this or Red now. He was going to stand up and face his old man.

Dick got up and started walking toward the door. The sheriff had managed to get to his side and watched Dick as he was leaving. He started to holler at Dick not to leave him like this, he'd bleed to death and Dick would be held responsible for it. He turned and looked at the sheriff who was still flapping his gums until he looked at Dick.

What he saw shut him up. Dick held the blade in his hand; his face was drawn and tight. The sheriff saw, or thought he saw, two red orbs where Dick's eyes should have been. The red rage had taken over Dick. The sheriff was the first person to see it, but not the last. Don't know which was redder, the sheriff's blood from a sliced nose or Dick's temper.

The door of the jailhouse slammed shut behind the freed boy. As he crept away from the vile place, he thought he heard a whimper coming from inside as the door closed, but he didn't care. He was free and he ran. With the "toothpick" still held tightly in his hand, Dick took off in the direction of the woods. He ran hard and his speed could have been only matched by a racehorse. The faster and further he ran, his outlook quieted, softened, and the rage finally subsided leaving him giddy and tired. He heaved a couple of deep breaths and stumbled a little bit. Then he stopped and sucked in the still warm, fall air to fill his lungs. He caught his breath and set out toward Red's place.

Dick snaked his way down hollows, over ridges, through creeks, and skirted the underbrush of his woods and found himself at the place he'd popped old Red. Up the hill and behind Red's barn, Dick slowed to a grinding halt. He didn't want to let on to anyone or any of the barn's residents that he was around. With the stealth he used when he hunted deer, Dick maneuvered toward the house. It was dark enough now that the light from the house left long shadows on the ground below the windows. Dick knew where Red's room was and moved to that part of the house. Red's light was on, too. There was an old maple tree that was limb heavy on the side of the house that Red occupied, so it made the perfect ladder to get up to Red's room and it still had enough leaves on it to cover Dick's ascent.

Dick hit that tree like a monkey who was hungry for a banana. Even with the pain from his ordeal at the sheriff's, he climbed the tree so fast he almost missed the limb that would let him into Red's room so he slowed down. He sat on the limb and let everything get quiet. Sitting for several minutes, he tried to figure out what he'd say to Red. He couldn't really come up with anything good. So he shrugged his shoulders and inched his way toward Red's window.

The room was lit, but silent. Dick thought that maybe Red was asleep. But as he stuck his head in the window, he noticed Red was sitting up sort of sideways with a bunch of pillows at his back. He was reading a book. Red was so intent on reading the book, he didn't even notice Dick when the unexpected intruder was standing behind him looking over his shoulder. Dick looked at the page Red was so interested in. His gaze fell on this passage.

"Three things return not, even for prayers and tears-The arrow which the archer shoots at will; The spoken word, keen-edged and sharp to sting; the opportunity left unimproved. If thou would'st speak a word of loving cheer, Oh speak it now. This moment is thine own." Dick knew at that moment that he had to say something.

"Red!" Dick whispered loudly. Red almost jumped out of his skin. He turned three shades of red and they all matched his hair.

"Dick, what in blazes are you doing here? My father would skin you alive if he knew you were here." Dick put his index finger to his mouth that gestured to Red to be quiet. Then, he came around to the side of the bed and sat on the edge.

"Red, old hoss, I'm sorry I shot you, but you pissed me off about what you said and I couldn't help myself. Something came over me and I went crazy. I'm sorry."

"That's okay, Dick. I know you wouldn't have done it if I hadn't taunted you in school and all. Anyway, I'm okay except when I have to take a dump, then having to go to the outhouse and sitting in that cold, hard, old seat, I want to shoot you." Both boys laughed and then caught each other's signal to be quiet.

Dick told Red what happened and that the sheriff was going to get Red to swear it was Dick who shot him. Red told Dick that the sheriff could go to hell before he'd squeal. Dick patted Red on the shoulder and said he had to go and again how sorry he was. Red just shook his head okay.

Dick got up to leave and turned to Red again and said, "I've been thinking about what all you said to me Red, and there's one thing you didn't say...that I was ugly. I appreciate that. I know my looks are hard. My father told me once that I was so ugly that a dog would close its eyes before it would hump my leg." Both boys almost busted out with laughter, but managed to control themselves.

Dick glanced at the book Red was reading and asked Red what it was about. Red blushed and tried to hide the book under one of the pillows on the bed. Dick was too fast for Red and snatched the book from the injured boy's hand. Dick stood up and looked at the front cover. *Poems from Anonymous Authors.*

"Alright smart guy, who was this Anonymous? One of those old Greeks we read about in class?" Red smiled and told Dick that it was something like that, then went on to explain to Dick that anonymous actually meant, "unknown." Dick flushed a little at that, but he shook it off. Red told him to take the book and read some of the poems and when they saw each other again, they could talk about them. Dick closed the book and told Red it was time he lit out. Dick walked to the window and halfway through it, he thanked Red for the book again.

He and Red looked eye to eye just long enough for the bond to be restored. Dick knew inside that Red was going to be his friend and Red knew Dick was going to be his friend. That was that. Dick shimmied down that tree as fast as a squirrel chased by a hound dog. He had tucked the book into a pocket in the front of his overalls and away from his knives. He was heading toward his momma's and when he got there, he didn't want to have anything keeping him from pulling the blade that made him any man's equal.

After quietly making his way, Dick came upon his home. The dirty yellow light from the kitchen fell onto the night's darkness like a splash of old paint. Dick skittered around to the back door and heard his old man.

"You stupid bitch. How am I going to hold my head up in town now that that bastard of a son of yours has gone and killed a child. Huh? How?" Dick heard the sound of his mother's face being slapped. His eyes began to fill again with the "rage."

Immediately, he jumped up on the steps and ran into the kitchen. Dick saw his old man hovering over his momma. One arm was raised high above his head and his hand was poised to slap her again. Dick fingered the "toothpick." His old man saw him and dropped his hand. He stared at Dick with a hard cold stare of a drunk that was on his way to being all drunk in a stupor. But, he was still coherent enough to channel his anger and think about the moves he'd need to make to exact the correct amount of punishment on this new victim.

Dick went to the side of his mother. Bessie sucked in gobs of air and snot between the sobs of her crying. She held her face in hand and the enclosure made her sound like a suckling pig squealing in a sack. Dick patted her with his left hand, all the while keeping his right hand on the hilt of his "toothpick." His old man fumed with eyes that were blood red from the consumption of the local "shine" he'd gotten that night. Standing there looking at Dick, his face got hotter and hotter while his anger grew. Dick had no shortage of fury himself. The two equaled their vengeance.

"You son of a bitch!" he shouted. "You bastard fucking son of a bitch!" He lunged for Dick who quickly sidestepped past the old man. When the young boy whirled by him, he turned around fast and was ready to run Dick down again. This time Dick was also ready; ready with the "toothpick." The old man didn't see the blade as he took off across the room toward Dick like he was doing ninety miles an hour. Dick came up with a high arching motion that caught the old man's belt, then his shirt, and angled the blade toward his right shoulder. Still drunk and unsteady, his father pulled up short and threw all his weight onto the balls of his feet and sucked in his stomach to keep the "pick" from gutting him. He tried to slap the knife away from Dick, but ended up cutting the side of his own hand. Dick stood his ground, but turned around when his old man's momentum propelled him past Dick.

Turning again, this time his father arched his back in order to stretch like the bulls do in the fighting rings in Mexico. After the toreadors impale them to get them angry, they bleed the bulls before the matador takes to the arena. Dick had no cape, but he had a "sword." The old man stood there bleeding from his wounds. Their eyes met. Four cold, steel blue eyes locked in a Cain and Able struggle.

Bessie, sitting on the floor where she was when Dick had come home, shook her head in horror. She stood up and let both of her arms fall to her sides. She clenched her fist so tight, air couldn't pass through her fingers. She threw her head back and screamed at the top of her lungs. This scream was a soulful noise meant to shake those with souls, but the two locked in this test of will had no souls to speak of anymore. Bessie then fainted and as she fell, she came between the two stone figures breaking the thoughts and tugging at the heart of just one of these men.

Suddenly distracted, Dick dropped his knife and

half-assed caught Bessie as she fell. The old man moved in on Dick while he was kneeling to lay his mother on the floor. With his speed and deliberation, Dick snatched the knife by its hilt, pulling it from the board where the balance of the knife's weight made it stick in the floor. The determined boy looked at the old man and saw that the onslaught had stopped as fast as it had begun. The wounds the old man had sustained were beginning to take their toll and the old man knew it.

Dick returned to the care of his mother and paid no more attention to his father. The old man backed up when Dick stood. He fell-sat into a kitchen chair. Heaving in air, the drunk let his arms hang loose by his sides. The pools of blood increased at each drop from his cuts. Dick went to the sink and pumped some water onto a dishrag. He then went to a cabinet along the wall of the kitchen where it went into the dining room. He opened the cabinet door and took out a jar of pickled eggs. With the rag and the jar of eggs, Dick kneeled down by his mother and opened the jar.

The acid smell combined with the pickling spice made him blow and turn his head a little. He took the top of the jar and waved it under his mother's nose. She jerked and sputtered. When her eyes sprang open, she was disoriented to the point she pulled away from her concerned son. Dick grabbed her and pulled her to him wiping her brow with the cold, wet rag. She smiled at Dick and took one of his hands in hers.

Holding it to her cheek, she said in a faint voice, "Always my Dick. My dear, dear boy."

The old man had finally bled enough that he was feeling faint. He slunk down in the chair, and then slid to the floor. Bessie saw him lying in his blood and told Dick to help her up. Dick did as he was told and helped his mother up from the floor. She staggered a little, but managed to straighten herself up a little. She took a deep breath and started to walk toward the old man. Dick called to her, but she paid him no attention.

Picking up the rag Dick had used to soothe her brow, she went to the sink and pumped fresh water into a pan and washed out the rag. She took the pan and clean rag to the old man's side. With almost caring motions, she began to clean the blood from the old man's wounds and told her son to get her sewing kit from under the counter. Dick stood there dumbfounded, transfixed in disbelief that his mother would lift a finger to help this old bastard. She hollered at Dick and the sound of her voice startled him from his train of thought, so instinctively he moved to do her bidding. He delivered the sewing kit and Bessie took a needle and white thread out telling him to get her some of the old man's hooch from the bedroom. Dick hesitated.

" Shoo now, go get the corn like I said!" was her response to his hesitation.

Again, he did his mother's bidding and brought back a jar full of the clear "devil" that caused them so many hours of misery. Bessie put the needle and thread into the jar with the hooch, knowing that the alcohol would sterilize them. She continued to clean the wounds and had Dick prop up the old man. When Bessie removed the sewing material from the jar, she poured some of the fire onto the wounds. The old man jumped and cussed a word or two when the juice entered his gashes.

"Don't waste that on my outsides, woman," he scowled. He told her to give him a drink. Dick gently stopped her hand as she was about to raise it to his lips. She looked at Dick, a sideways look, and moved her hand away from his. Dick knew then that there was no way he had won anything for her. She was still a slave to the old man and of her own choice. Dick shook his head in disbelief and pity for her, but he knew he had shown his old man that now it would take more than a mean cruel, old man to keep

Dick down. The old coot would not ever abuse him again. Bessie started to coo at her husband telling him he'd be alright and talking for Dick as to how sorry he was and he didn't mean to do what he'd done to him. Dick stood next to his mother and his stomach turned as he heard her words. He couldn't stand it any longer and turned to leave the kitchen walking, slowly at first then, picking up speed, he took off out the back door. Quickly, he headed to the "hole" and his sanctuary. He had to figure all this out; the anger, the betrayal by his mother, all of it, *all of it.*

Dick got to the "hole" and entered the darkness as one would a lighted room. He took the lamp from its place and the matches from the shelf above the cot. The sound the long arch made from the match, overshadowed the sound of the hissing gas from the lamp. Then, there was a slight popping sound when the flame of the match ignited the lamp and the darkness raced toward the corners of the room. Dick sat the lamp on the table and flopped down onto the cot. The physical strain of the day's events had taken their toll on this man-child. With slumping shoulders and sleep pushing the last moments of awareness from his beleaguered mind, Dick sat on the edge of the cot as though he were trying to squeeze himself into a ball. His mind beat him up more and more as he sat there in spite of the fact that he wanted to just drift off and sleep. No such luck. The images of the fight between him and his father teased his body by making the pressure behind his eyes build and fall, build and fall, causing him to have a headache as big as a mule's butt.

Dick moved his body and fell back onto the cot and his right hand felt the book Red had let him have. His first thought was to hurl the *intruder* across the room to slap the far wall. The book didn't make the noise Dick thought it would. Instead of a slap, all he heard was a thud and the book falling to the floor. He made himself get up from the cot and retrieve the object of his temper. As he ambled over to the opened tome and turned it over to the open pages, his headache abated somewhat as he began to read a passage from the book,

"That they may minister to the desire of thy heart:
For at length that day of lamentation shall come
Wherein he whose heart is still shall not hear the
lamentation,
Never shall cries of grief cause
To beat again the heart of a man who is in the
grave.
Therefore occupy thyself with thy pleasure daily,
And never cease to enjoy thyself."

Dick took the book, went back to the table, and sat down on the box he used as a stool. His mind eagerly ate each word from the pages before him. He read until his eyes hurt and putting aside the book, he lay down on the cot and started to doze off. When sleep finally overcame him, his mind, that normally would have tormented him with visions of his mother and father, was filled with the words of unknown writers who had left their messages to the world to do with what it would. Dick's dreams were filled with the words of Jesse James, Water Boy, Absence, Texas Rangers, A Spartan's Death, and many more. Some of these narratives left him wanting, saddened him, empowered him for tomorrow, but best of all, they made him sleep.

The loud volume of the tape ending and the snow on the TV screen appearing after listening to Ce for so long, made me jump. Janet was massaging her tired hand trying to get rid of the cramps. I stood up and moved to turn the machines off. The phone rang. I immediately looked at Janet and she at me. It rang about five times before I just grabbed it.

"Hello."

"Mr. Ce has two more tapes for you to watch. Don't leave the condo. Please begin watching again at 12:30 a.m. . . ." The caller hung up the phone. I did, too. I stood there staring at the damn thing for what seemed to be hours. Janet asked me who was on the phone. Awakened from my daze, I said it sounded like "Snid." She asked what the hell did he want? I told her what he'd said. She frowned.

"I've got to get out of this room. I'm going stir crazy listening to him drone on and on and we've got to sit through two more of these damn tapes? Please, please, please, let's get out of here for awhile." With the tremor in her voice and the way her eyes looked, all sad and longing, I could not say no. My manly voice spoke up in my head and popped out with, the hell with this mumbo jumbo voodoo bullshit. The important thing is to keep this real live person happy. Amen! I told Janet to get dressed in some comfortable clothes and we would split before the "booga booga" called and stopped us.

We were dressed and out of the condo in nothing flat. The dreaded heat and humidity this time was a blessing. We were free from the haints. We took off toward the "square" and decided to pick up a carriage ride to see some of the sights. We'd planned to do this anyway, but all our original plans were scrapped because of the hoodoo and the murders. When we got to the square, the carriages were all full or pulling away from the overhanging tree branches that shielded them from the sun each time they waited for more tourists.

We saw one left and hurried to catch it before someone else made a beeline to it. The driver was feeding the horse from a feedbag and when we approached him, he told us he was off duty now, and Genevieve here must rest and eat. I was sweating like a sieve and didn't want to listen to, "no", from anyone. I stood there looking at Janet and saw the disappointment in her face. I reached down and drew a handful of water from the concrete trough wiping my face and the back of my neck. The cool tepid water felt good.

I said, "Okay. How much will it take for you and Ms. Genevieve to cut lunch short and give me and my wife the grand tour?" I waited a minute for some outrageous amount to come out of the driver's mouth.

He spoke up and said, "Genevieve does not work unless she wants to mon ami, n'est-ce pas. Entre nous she has idee fixe about these things. Sometimes though, if someone has the savoir faire when they approach her, she may change her mind."

"How would we know if she changed her mind?"

"Easy mon ami, she will act ah, san souci, how you say, 'care free' and then, voila, the deal is done."

"Great," I said. "Then, how much to take the ride?"

"First things first, mon ami. Please talk to my Genevieve and see if you can persuade her to be your guide." I got a quick little nudge from Janet and approached the horse rather cautiously considering the task.

"Okay, horse. Do you want to take us or not?" There was no response for a moment, then the horse raised its tail and let the world know her response. Big green blobs of horse turds hit the hot pavement.

"Mon ami, you are not the one to get my little one happy with such harsh talk. You need the bon mot, entre nous, she may respond better from the voice of the pretty lady."

I looked to Janet and said, "You're up." Janet gave me her "okay, smarty" look, stepped up to the horse, and began to pet and rub the horse's nose and under its jaws. Janet leaned in to the horse's right ear and said something soft enough that I couldn't hear. The horse swung its head up and gave one of those goofy horse laughs and then put her head on Janet's shoulder.

The driver said, "And voila, we have the one. The ladies have had their tete a' tete."

"Okay," I snapped. "How much is this going to cost me?"

"For you and the enchanting lady, I will let you ride a bon marche, mon ami."

"Which is?" I asked.

"$20.00," he responded. I looked at Janet and the deal was done since she had bonded with the horse. Old *Mr. Ed* tunes began to fill my mind, "a horse is a horse of course, of course, da da da." Whatever! The driver lowered the little step on the side of the carriage and in somewhat of an old world bow, said, "Bien venu." Not being, as they say, au fait in Cajun or French, I muddled through most of what the driver had thrown at me by shaking my head and smiling. I just wanted to get on the damn thing and have whatever little breeze this thing could muster up hit me so I would quit melting.

I let Janet climb in and then I got up and sat next to her. The driver got on board and with his back to us, he took the reins and gently told the horse to go. When the hooves began to clop, the movement of the carriage stirred a little breeze and I cooled down a bit. Janet sat quietly with a bright smile on her face.

She spoke to the driver and asked him what his name was. He squared his shoulders and said something in French about a mile long and then informed us that here, in the city, he was known as Bee Chee. Janet spoke up and told him we were the Madisons. He nodded his recognition and continued driving.

As we sauntered along, he began to tell us, in a mixture of English, French, and Cajun, the history of the old city and the characters that played and still play a part of the city's mystique. As he kept on with his discourse, Janet and I were past the slight breeze stage and were baking quite nicely in the heavy humidity and sun.

I interrupted Bee Chee during one of his canned spiels about the old graveyard and the famous Voodoo queen buried there, to ask him if there was a place we could stop and get some water or a coke or something. He must not have liked interrupting his routine. He shot me a look. You know, one of those !@#$$ looks.

Janet saw all of this, reached up, and touched his arm to say, "Please, for me and Genevieve…"

I saw his demeanor change when he nodded and turned around to face the front again and said, "For the ladies."

Well great, I had been out of the condo no more than an hour and I had already pissed somebody off and a large animal had taken a shine to my wife. *Ain't this precious.* I felt like griping, but I put my arm around Janet instead. There was no need to let the small stuff get to me.

Bee Chee didn't say much any more at least until we veered off the main drag and headed out of the city. I, of course, was trying to find a rock to suck on to keep from dehydrating. Janet was perspiring, but I was sweating the Mississippi. Usually, I have taken heat pretty well, but today, damn. I guessed Bee Chee was so accustomed to this extreme, he wouldn't lose a drop of moisture in hell.

The road we were on led us through the countryside and past old hulks of plantations. These once proud landmarks of the past were now dead themselves, slowly rotting to rejoin the earth. They were fading like the past.

Genevieve plodded along and her head began to droop now and again. I was getting hotter and was just about to say something, when the horse, along with the carriage, decided to take a side road, stirring up dust along with some nasty mosquitoes. All around us was swamp and old, black water slues, the kind you see in movies where the gators are all out to eat the human invaders. It was beautiful, but I preferred to be in a nice air-conditioned room with a cold glass of water looking at all this on the tube. Between the heat and our wandering, I was irritated.

After a few minutes of following the side road, Janet spoke to Bee Chee about the water and asked exactly where we were going. Genevieve again pulled off in the direction heading directly into the sun and it was so bright, even with shades on, it was difficult to see clearly. The carriage finally pulled under a large weeping willow that had probably been there since Adam and Eve were kicked out. This tree was big and Spanish moss hanging from the already dangling branches made a great cover and heat barrier.

Janet and I looked at each other and sighed when the shady temperature registered and the cool of the area hit us full force. Bee Chee jumped from the carriage and went to the large trunk he had on the back and opened it. He moved as though he were angry, but pulled two bottles of something from the trunk. The bottles had droplets of moisture on them as though they had been kept in a cooler. I asked, if in fact, the trunk was a cooler and he said yes. I thought to myself that all this time we were parched, this guy had cold water. What a rip. He handed a bottle to Janet and then to me. He muttered something in French and I popped the top off my bottle and chugged it down. Janet took a small sip. I sucked mine down as fast as a politician goes through campaign funds at election time. The only addition I could ask for that relief was more of the same.

The coldness of the liquid hit my stomach and I immediately felt my whole body tingle and I stopped perspiring. I sighed and sat way back in the carriage seat. All this took less than a minute. I looked at Janet to see how she was coming with her water and I saw her spitting it out. She grabbed my arm as she looked for Bee Chee; he was nowhere to be found. Then it hit me. My gut rolled and my brain started convulsing. I was tripping. Whatever was in that bottle sure wasn't water. I was sitting down so I guess I was lucky. Janet must have sat on me while I was hallucinating.

The things I imagined, so Janet tells me, were many and varied. She told me later that I first screamed passages from the Bible, especially Revelations. After Revelations, I intoned some of the book of John. Days later I looked it up, the chapter, and as close as I could come to one of the passages Janet remembered, it was from John 7:24, "Do not judge according to appearance, but judge with righteous judgment." She also told me that I recited poems.

The one she remembered was a poem I'd read in a book my father had given me years ago called, *Song of the Harper*. The passage I blurted out was, "Behold a man is not permitted, to carry his possessions away with him. Behold there never was anyone who, having departed, was able to come back again." I don't know why this crap came so easily from my head, but there it was and there we were.

During all my blathering, Janet had her hands full. It seems Genevieve decided to follow Bee Chee to wherever he took off. Janet had to keep a tight reign on the horse, and at the same time, keep me from running and screaming blah blahs into the swamp. Since I was as loony as a Dodo during this time, I'm going to let Janet fill in the missing parts of this particular situation.

David, as he's mentioned, was not himself for most of this adventure. He's turning up his nose to the reference

*that our experience was an "adventure," but hey, I'm
telling this part and to me it was an adventure.*

Citing poetry and biblical verse in David's
ramblings was due to constant reading on his part.
Concepts and words stay with him and he holds them
inside. I guess that's one of the reasons he doesn't drink.
He doesn't want to lose control over his emotions. He's
extremely reluctant about trusting people. He said to me
once that in the Bible, it says that God respects no man, and
if God did that, who was he to do something different?

So there I was, in a swamp in a carriage, with an
ultra-stoned 240-pound man trying to stay focused and
keep us from ending up snake-bitten and gator food. I
slipped David's belt from around his waist and secured one
hand and then the other. With the belt I had left, I tied it
around the handrail of the carriage and this kept him from
getting out of the carriage and running off. I got the reigns
and stopped Genevieve from wandering deeper into the
swamp. For a brief moment, it seemed that I had a handle
on the situation. I looked around from the carriage seat and
tried to get my bearings. The sun was setting. And darkness
fell fast in areas where the artificial light of the city didn't
penetrate to give off a glow. I was hoping we were not too
far from civilization and I could get Genevieve to head
back into a more inhabited part of the countryside, at least
to an area where I could call an ambulance for David. I was
worried that he may have swallowed too much of whatever
it was in that bottle and would become brain-fried into a
zombie-stoned freak forever.

I shook off that maudlin thought and tied the reigns
to a tree. I then went around to the big carriage trunk and
opened it to see if there was anything in there that we could
eat or drink. I knew not to drink anything from a bottle that
looked like the ones Bee Chee gave us. To my surprise the
trunk contained a couple of sandwiches, an oat bag for the

horse, and a couple of two liter cola bottles that had water in them. I took one of these bottles and poured some of the water into an old bucket hanging from a loop tied to the side of the trunk. I remembered what David had told me about horses and any other animal, that they wouldn't drink tainted water unless they were dying. Too bad he didn't know about this before he downed the stuff Bee Chee gave us. I filled the bucket with the water and took it to the horse. She looked at me with what I think was gratitude, then she stuck her head into the bucket and began to drink. I let her finish and then I brought her the oat bag.

David was still floundering around and I couldn't get any water in him. I was hungry and thirsty with a sneaking suspicion it was going to be a long night so I ate part of a sandwich and drank a few sips of water. I held David's head between my knees and dripped water into his mouth from my handkerchief.

The night engulfed us quickly and I began to hear the sounds of the swamp fill the ever-increasing darkness. I really couldn't see anything past my nose so I took pepper spray from my purse and kept it near me. I followed David's body until I found one of his knives and I took it from its holder putting it next to my pepper spray. I didn't know if I could use it the way David did, but it gave me comfort. I knew he had two or three more on him, so if he got his head back, he'd be okay.

I hit the indigo on my watch and saw it was about 7:30p.m. David finally quit floundering and from his heavy snoring and breathing, I knew he was out like a light. The bugs were horrible. The mosquitoes were coming in droves and other blood-sucking things were attacking the horse. I could feel the swish of air from her tail and she grunted in pain from something biting her now and again. It was all I could do to fan David and try to keep myself from being eaten alive.

The hours passed and I tried to stay awake. Even with the bugs, I caught myself dozing off. I was just about fast asleep when I saw a light, faint and yellow. It came from the swamp side of the carriage and I thought I was seeing things at first. I controlled my urge to yell out. David's mentoring had taken hold and in any situation he has always warned, "If it seems too good to be true, it usually is." I waited until I could see the light bearer and possibly anyone else. It took forever for what appeared to be a few people to get out of the swamp. I heard a lot of murmuring and then solid words filtered through, but it was all in Cajun and pidgin French. I sounded out the words I could understand and what I heard scared me. These people had been sent to get us and take us to some priest or someone in charge. They had to hurry and get us back before the ceremony began.

Being a fan of the old classic horror films, I always thought that if I ever saw anything in real life that I had seen on screen, I could explain it to myself. What I saw coming toward me was straight out of the celluloid tombs. Nine of the most disheveled and sickly looking men I'd ever seen came lumbering out of that swamp. In the lead was our driver Bee Chee. He looked like someone had dragged him through the shit pile and stuck him in the sun to dry. The light from the torch he was carrying made me take a second look, but from the position I was in all the freaks looked alike. I had my hand on the pepper spray and David's knife. If nothing else, I'd protect us for a second or two. David would be proud of me.

I hunkered over him to give the impression that I was out, too. I heard the swamp men getting closer. They shuffled as they came and it seemed hours before they got to us. I felt the pull on the handrail and Genevieve lurched as one of the men tried to get on board. My plan was to jump up and spray them with the pepper, brandishing the knife and try to scare them away. Surprise was a weapon.

I gathered all my strength to move, then an iron hand grasped me from the seat of the carriage. Startled, I stared into David's face. In the garish torchlight, I saw recognition beaming from his face. I stopped my attack when I saw him give me his "wait" look. I settled down in the hunkered over position and kissed him on the forehead. When I did, I felt an eyelid open and close against my chin. In a garbled accent, one of the men said to Bee Chee that we were passed out. During all of this, Genevieve was snorting and trying to get away from the strangers. I heard Bee Chee talk to her in soothing terms and she settled down. He made the "nec, neck" sound and then the carriage began to move forward. I saw the outline of a figure sitting in the front on the driver's seat. It was Bee Chee.

He said to Genevieve, "I knew these were special people, my sweet, and so did you. We are attuned little one. These people have the 'idee fixe' to do and go where they want even if it may mean their lives, n'est-ce pas?"

I jerked when I heard the "lives" part. A strong hand kept me down. I moved my other hand slowly and patted David on the arm. He lightened his grip. He knew I was cool for a while.

The horse and carriage continued on into the darkness. I suppose the "walkers" that came with Bee Chee headed back into the swamp. The ride was somewhat smooth for a few minutes then we began to bounce around quite a bit. I guessed we'd gotten off the "dirt" road and headed into the swamp. The wheels made the carriage shake and slide around as if we were in old wheel ruts. David was bouncing around more than I was because of the way I had tied him to the handrail. I guess Bee Chee thought that if both of us were "out" he needn't check on how we were doing in the seats. I felt for David's belt and undid the knot I'd made and I felt his arms silently go past me. I had no doubt that he'd gotten one of his knives, probably the one he always carried in his boot. That knife was his favorite. It had belonged to his father.

A few more minutes passed and I was so sweaty and sticky, I knew when we stopped there would be hell to pay if anyone let me get any hotter. My light pink cotton blouse was sticking to me and I hoped my bra wouldn't show too badly if there was any bright light. We began to hear voices and something of a commotion going on, then streaks of torch light flickered past the carriage. We came to a halt and people began to mill about the carriage. I kept my eyes at a slit to try and get a look at who was around us. Bee Chee stood up with a whip in his hand and shouted to these people to leave us alone or taste the "sting of the master's whip." The crowd backed away and low murmuring was all I could hear. I was just about to raise my head when David touched the toe of my foot and I stopped my movement.

Bee Chee jumped from the driver's seat and shouted for someone named Po'lare. He told him to remove me from the carriage and get a couple of the "zombies" to get the man. At the word "zombie", my fingers tightened around the pepper spray and I quickly opened the knife. I was too hot and bug bitten to let some "zombie" pick me up or possibly hurt David while he was unable to protect us. The seconds passed and I heard the footfalls of someone coming to the carriage. I supposed it to be this Po'lare. At reaching the sidestep, this person called loudly to the crowd in some language I thought was Jamaican. I heard other footfalls coming to the carriage. I waited like David had always coached me to do if a situation occurred where surprise would be the key to getting out of a mess.

Suddenly, as the weight of the stranger pulled on the carriage, David jumped up and screamed, "Hey, asshole, didn't anyone ever tell you, never eat anything bigger than your own head?"

With that off the wall comment, I knew he had gained his mind again. That sarcasm was from a book by a guy named Kliban. It was full of stuff like that. David loved to play head games with jerks by using quotes from the books he had collected by that author. The pregnant pause was enough to leave Bee Chee and his freaks standing with open mouths and total stupidity on their faces.

David looked at me urgently and said, "Now!"

I jumped up and screamed something to the effect of, "Do you want fries with your pepper spray, sir?"

With that I let the spray stream right into Po'lare's eyes and he fell from the step. The two other "zombies" backed off while David and I quickly stepped off the carriage standing back to back, circling, and watching the crowd of freaks. He and I both kept crouched and were ready.

Right at that instant of impending danger, a booming baritone voice came from the back of the crowd of dips and these guys fell over each other trying to make a hole for whoever was coming. A tall figure with a top hat on his head and a bunch of bones around his neck came wading through. He was holding a staff of sorts with a beautifully carved shaft of African symbols. He proceeded to yell something that sounded like a threat. Two of the "zombies" started toward us, one from each side. David cautioned me to concentrate on what I'd been taught about using a knife. This was for real. I'd never used a knife, but I was ready that night.

One of the misbegotten "zombies" lunged at David as I felt his body move with practiced grace and heard the knife find its target. It was a hard sound. David must have used the hilt of his knife. I know the sound of the "long death." My own assailant moved to within an arm's length and I sidestepped him as he went to the side of me. When he bolted forward, I slashed at him and at the same time I tripped him. He hit the ground like a sack of potatoes and didn't move. I'd just killed the man, a human being. Every moral fiber in my body screamed at me. I had committed a sin; I'd killed. I almost dropped the knife and fell to my knees to ask forgiveness for what I'd done. For a moment, I just stood there.

David's voice boomed at me. "Snap out of it, honey. It's them or us." I regained my composure. *Them or us, them or us.* I kept repeating those words in my head.

The JuJu man yelled again and this time Bee Chee pushed more "zombies" toward us. I saw Po'lare wiping his eyes and knew he was still having problems.

David said, "Honey, these 'zombies' are harmless. Let's get Bee Chee and the big guy so these spooks will disappear." I yelled an Okay! We started toward them. Bee Chee was whipping the air over and over with the buggy whip, scaring the 'zombies" and yelling at them to move in on us. David kicked one in the groin and elbowed another. I sprayed one and he yelped like a dog and started running. He ran smack dab into old Po'lare and the two of them hit the dirt. David confronted them and the crowd of freaks made a circle as fast as their shuffling feet would allow them. I made sure they were far enough away from me by brandishing the knife and the spray.

No sound came from the crowd once the circle had been formed. The two antagonists faced each other, one with a knife the other with a buggy whip. David got into his fighting stance. Bee Chee began to circle David flicking the whip in a high arch. All those "zombie" eyes were glued on them. My eyes were on the JuJu man. David had told me years ago that where there was more than one leader of a group, the tactic was to engage one of the prey while the other leader pulled a sneak attack and usually the prey was a goner, so always keep a eye open for the second one. It could save your life.

David was right. The JuJu man was circling behind the crowd and trying to get behind David. I pushed my way through the wall of bodies and met him face to face as he was coming around on the left. It surprised him so much, he dropped his pistol. When he did, I sprayed him in the face and he dropped his pretty stick. I scooped it up and broke it over his top hat. Too bad for him, the hat was still attached to his head. He fell to his knees, then went face down in the dirt. I snatched up the pistol and I pushed my way back into the crowd. I saw David hanging on to the whip while he and Bee Chee were doing a dance. Bee Chee would pull at the whip and David would pull back and swing his knife at Bee Chee. I didn't have any doubt that David was playing with Bee Chee. David looked at me and I nodded I was all right. He must have seen I had gone for awhile.

At my nod, David pulled the whip so hard that Bee Chee ended up two inches from David's face. As if struck dumb, Bee Chee just stood there. David yelled, "That's all folks." He turned the blade away from Bee Chee and struck him in the face with the hilt. Bee Chee fell backward with a thud. As David predicted, the "zombies" began to scatter. Even the one I thought I'd killed pushed himself halfway off the ground. When he got a toehold on solid ground, he took off. David and I stood there a minute watching the mob heading away from us. Bee Chee and JuJu man were still out for the count.

I threw an arm around David. He picked me up and swung me around as though we were at a dance. When my feet felt earth again, he kissed me so hard I thought for a second he was about to break my teeth. Instead of caving in, I pressed back and, and, well it was just the greatest kiss ever! While we were embracing David must have felt the pistol I'd stuck in the waistband of my shorts. He gingerly removed it and treated it like a hot potato.

"Very funny," I said.

"A Glock 9. JuJu boys were packing some mean fire power," David commented with gratitude in his voice that it wasn't used on us. He kicked at Bee Chee then. When he didn't stir, David removed the rope from around Bee Chee"s waist, tied his hands to his feet and then we headed toward JuJu man.

"Good job, honey," David complimented. I flushed, a bit embarrassed and happy at the same time. David was pleased. He picked up one of the torches the mob had dropped as they scattered. As he bent down close to JuJu man, he asked me to roll him over. With one hand holding the pistol and the other the torch, he could have moved JuJu, but it would be safer if I did it. JuJu was big, but I managed to get a good foothold and then I rolled him. The face that greeted us was hard and blank of expression. David poked him with the barrel of the gun. He didn't move. I checked his pulse and he was still breathing, thank God. David lowered the torch and moved it over the body like he was a copying machine. I asked him what he was looking for. He told me he had read about this kind of shaman or priest. If his memory wasn't playing tricks on him, a person of that status was marked with the runes of a practitioner of the black arts of voodoo.

"Well, do the markings tell you if he was any good at what he practiced?"

David looked at me with a half smile and said, "By the markings on his chest and stomach, along with the symbols on the rune stick you so unceremoniously broke over his skull, this puppy is supposedly so bad, he could spit in the devil's eye and get an big E for effort."

I looked at the body, then David, and finally after peering at the runes on the stick, the observations David had made were beginning to get creepy. I looked back at him with a longing to say *bull shit*, instead I inquired that if this guy was solo bad, why was he carrying a pistol?

David flinched. He pulled me down behind him and looked beyond the faltering light the torch put out and sniffed the air. Something or someone was there. I fingered the pepper spray and made sure the knife was still with me. A voice from the edge of the swamp called out.

"Ho' there David, it's just old Ce." Being so close to David, I felt him tense again. It was Ce, wasn't it? I whispered into David's ear that it was Ce and told him to calm down. David, still looking at the area where the voice emanated from whispered, "Calm's ass."

Then suddenly he shouted, "Come out of the swamp with your hands up, and do it slowly. Don't let your imagination become overactive at this juncture." I jumped out of my skivvies. David rolled and pointed the pistol toward the dark where the voice and statement came from. He didn't fire. I moved over and got behind David.

At that point, the voice declared, "Do I sound so different in real life than on a video tape?" It was Ce alright. But David still kept the pistol pointed at the voice.

"Come on out, nice and slow, with your hands above your head," he commanded. I looked over at David and the expression on his face was that of someone who believes in their sixth sense, but then again doesn't take any unnecessary chances.

Ce stepped out from the darkness, the shadows thrown by the torch played around his form. I saw and felt David tense as we both followed Ce's movements and swung my head back and forth to keep a sharp eye on David. I could have been watching a tennis match.

Ce appeared to move without moving. If you watch people when they walk, you can see them saunter, or goose step, or just put one foot in front of the other. People walk straight, bow legged, pigeon toed and knock kneed, but Ce, he floated. It must have been the heat, the shadows or something, because people don't float, right? He stood next to the writhing body of the JuJu man and with his cane poked at him. A squeamish cry came from the big hulk that lay on the ground before us. Ce walked over to Bee Chee and poked him with the cane. Bee Chee was bleeding from the wound he'd gotten when he and the hilt of the knife collided.

I swear it was either the excitement or the after effects of the tainted water I had consumed, but when the torch light struck Ce's face, I could see his nostrils flare and his tongue flicked across his lips like a snake's. He must have sensed I was watching him because he hurriedly gained his composure.

Quickly he turned to us and said, "Forgive me, the taste of evil sometimes is overpowering to me. It fills the air here as much as the perfume of the honeysuckle and jasmine that beautify this area."

Thinking it odd I hadn't noticed before, I took a deep breath at that comment and both the fragrances filled my lungs. I enjoyed the headiness of the fragrances until I caught the sour essence of something that reminded me of the way the morgue smelled. I almost wretched. David stood by and said nothing, pistol in hand. He later confided to me that even though he had his "head" back, he wasn't going to let his guard down until he was sure he was seeing and hearing actual beings.

With the pistol still held firm, David stepped right up to Ce and looked him square in the eyes. These two men stood toe to toe and so close, a breeze couldn't squeeze between them. I caught my breath in a big gulp and waited. I saw David's hand, the one holding the pistol, slowly point the barrel toward the ground. David shook his head from side to side as though he were shaking out cobwebs. He backed away from Ce. When he turned toward me, he had a tear in his eye. I put my hand to his face and brushed away that one lone tear.

He straightened up and turned to Ce asking, "What the hell are you doing here?"

Ce responded with, "Funny you mention hell, my boy. You may have been on your way to hell along with your beautiful wife. But, you're a Madison and can take care of yourself, can't you?"

David wanted to say something, but I guess he thought better of it. Ce dismissed the moment and continued.

"Enough. Let's take care of this evil trash and get you two back to the city, your condo, and the other tapes."

He held up his cane and a shadow moved from the edge of the swamp toward us. I stiffened and David moved into his fighting stance. I watched the shadow dart in and out of the light giving off its own shadow. It registered in my mind that the form was solid and not some unworldly creature summoned by Ce.

David explained out of the corner of his mouth, "It's Snid." I loosened up then, just a little. Snid's visage suddenly stood beside Ce. He told him to gather up the bodies of Bee Chee and the JuJu man and quietly place them in storage for their "just and timely" departure from this plane. Snid grabbed JuJu and Bee Chee by a heel and for such a small man, I was astonished upon muttering the softest grunt, he dragged both of these large deadweights away. We all watched as Snid disappeared into the swamp. Ce turned to us and said in a very deep and dry tone that it was time for us to remove ourselves from these, "haunts" and go back to the condo now.

David said, "And how do you propose we do this little feat? Grow wings and fly or would you have us walk back to town?"

Ce smiled a smile of someone who was trying not to get angry with a child. In a controlled voice, he stated that we would return to civilization the way we had arrived, in a carriage; specifically, the one we had come to the swamp in. I looked puzzled. David on the other hand had his "kiss my ass" look on his face. Ce's face showed that he was irritated. He raised his hand and pointed his index finger toward David. His hand shook as though he were nodding "yes" with it instead of his head. A slow, crisp smile played across his face. After what we had been through, we didn't need that.

Two defiant souls were pushing the envelope of tolerance. I had to do something before these two men who were allied in memories of another man, another time, tore at each other. So, I fainted. David called out my name as I began to crumple to the ground. His arm caught me and I proceeded to the ground, but as gently as a feather floating to a stop. He took out a handkerchief from his back pocket and dabbed the perspiration from my forehead. I kept my eyes closed and tried to picture in my mind the goings on around me.

Ce was telling Mr. Snid to bring the carriage and some water. I lay there with my head cradled in David's lap. Everything around me became silent. As the seconds passed, the weight of the swamp pressed down on all of us and suddenly I heard from both men, "Sorry."

At that I began to sputter and came out of my "vapors" and I told David to "please" get me home. The squeaking of the carriage wheels broke the silence of the moment and the shadowed Snid brought me some water. It was cold, but I hesitated a little about drinking some until Ce chuckled and told me it was bottled water from Arkansas. I downed it like a shooter. David helped me onto the carriage and Ce handed him the reigns.

"Just let Genevieve have her head and she'll get

you back to the city," Ce assured us. David reached for the leather straps Ce held up to him. His grasp on the reigns was strong and he did not let them go before he explained something to David.

"Please listen to me. There are things in this world, unseen things, things that you brush against, breath deep into your lungs, taste, smell, and even scratch, that are evil. Doors to other planes open and if a human is not careful or keenly aware, he or she can be sucked into the void and be lost in the chaos that breeds more evil. I am telling you to stay in your condo. Listen to the tapes. Write what you will, but stay behind those doors until we are done. I can only protect you for so long."

He let go of the straps. David looked at him in a way I never saw him look at any man. It was obvious to me he was humbled with submission.

With a light touch, David held on to the reigns and let Genevieve have her head as we leaned back into the carriage's deep leather seats. We were still drenched in our own perspiration and stuck to the leather like two flies on flypaper. I don't think we even cared. The night was waging war with the morning. The tell-tale signs of sunlight were pushing their way into the swamp. The sounds of insects and amphibians slowed as the quiet hour before the dawn surrounded us. I looked at David and saw his head was pushed back against the seat. His eyes were closed. I thought to myself that that was a good position to be in, so I laid back and shut my eyes and listened to the horse plod its way along the old road. David spoke so quietly I almost didn't hear him.

"Honey, I'm sorry I've gotten you into this mess." I put my fingers to his mouth to silence him.

"Hush now," I whispered softly.

The night's events rushed into my head and snippets of all the other things that had happened to us. I cringed at the thought of trying to make any sense of any of it. I peeled myself off the seat enough to lay my head in David's lap, then closed my eyes and let the mesmerizing sound of his breathing and the soft plod, plod, of Genevieve lull me to sleep.

In what seemed like almost an instant, David's voice was gently prodding me, "Honey, wake up" and I jumped up from his lap ready to fight all comers. "It's okay, Sweetie. We're back at the condo."

I shook the woolies from my head and looking around, I knew the night was over. The street was silent except for the few maintenance people who cleaned away the rude civilization dropped at night by the tourists in this city of the "Big Easy."

We got down from the carriage and stood there, both wondering what we were to do with Genevieve. Her head swung around to look at us. The big, sad horse met our eyes and then she whinnied and tossed her head high. When she pulled her head back down, she nuzzled me and I stroked her nose. She pulled away then and managed a stare at David as she began moving off with a known destination in mind. Her shoes made that hollow clopping sound that pavement and cobblestones bring. We stood there for a minute and then turned to go into the building.

The cold contrast from the air conditioned building rushed over us like a wave and I shuddered. We went directly to the room. After entering, David locked the door and put the deadbolt in place. He then slid a chair in front of the door and cocked it back so the top rest was under the doorknob. I was hit with a collective relief. I looked at him, he looked at me.

We came together, kissed and then almost simultaneously said, "Stinky."

I said, "Shower."

He said, "Coffee."

I went to the bathroom, he went to the kitchen. I turned the faucet on to let the hot water flow and in a few seconds, the door opened and David remarked that the, "soup" was on and cooking.

We disrobed and got under the rain of hot water and let the night slide off our bodies. The soap and shampoo removed the bug poop and dirt from our blotchy skin and also revealed all the bite marks we had collected. David grabbed me and I thought he would squeeze the life out of me. I giggled at first, but then realized that he was shivering. His face was buried in my shoulder and I thought I heard a faint cry. I pushed him in front of me and he stood there with his arms dangling, head down; the same way he stood in front of Ce. I thought perhaps it was a reaction to the drug he'd swallowed. I gently pulled back the shower curtain and cut off the water. The steam filled the room and it was as if we were moving in a heavy fog. I found a towel and handed it to him and took one for myself. I opened the bathroom door and the cold air rushed in to us.

"Come on, honey, let's get you some rest," I said. It was like leading someone whose will and strength had been drained. Although David was so tired he felt like a "zombie" himself, this one was mine and I was going to protect him as long as I had breath in me. I knew that if the situation was reversed, he'd do the same for me.

When I got him to the bed, I pulled back the covers and laid him down. As he felt the comforting sheets beneath him, his eyes shut tight. His knees pushed up toward his chest and I covered him. I got my robe on and spooned him. In a few minutes, I could feel and hear his breathing become deeper and his tension slowly dissipate. I too, fell asleep, but awoke somewhat startled. I had forgotten where I was and I didn't recall anything I dreamed. I slapped the pillow and was going to rollover and return to the land of sleep when it dawned on me,

David was gone. I jerked up and hollered his name. When I didn't get an answer, I jumped up and ran to the living room. A quick look told me he wasn't there.

Then I smelled the CDM brewing and a sweet smell of something cooking coming from the kitchen. David had the vent on and I guess he couldn't have heard me from the bedroom. I checked myself, hair okay, robe wrinkled, but passable, and a big smile.

"Hey, Sweetie," I greeted cheerfully.

He turned to me and held out his arms like he wanted a hug and I took him up on it. As we held each other, I could not help but think that something was still troubling him. I kissed his cheek and told him to go sit at the little table in the breakfast nook.

I poured two cups of coffee and opened the oven to find cinnamon rolls with the icing just starting to melt. I pulled them out of the oven, took a spatula, and scooped a half dozen onto a plate. Taking the plate and the coffee cups, I balanced them enroute to the table. David sat there with his head in his hands. I put everything down and looked at him warmly.

"Honey, what's wrong? Please talk to me."

He slowly raised his head and I saw a look of sorrow and regret on his face. I reached to him. He took a deep breath and exhaled. He stared for a moment searching for the right words, I guess.

He said, "I stood toe to toe with a man. I had a pistol and a knife, but what I saw in that man's eyes crushed my soul." I asked what he saw.

Another deep breath escaped from his lips and he said, "I saw them all; hate, anger, greed, lust, envy, deceit, betrayal; every nasty element that escaped from Pandora's box. Everything I saw had my face or what I thought was my face, but it changed so often in that short time, I don't know how it was all jammed together.

I saw two hands holding the book of life, but when the book opened and my name was not there, my soul screamed and my heart cried."

Chapter Eleven

I looked at Janet and I saw big tears well up in her eyes. I reached over and touched her knee. We leaned into each other and kissed. Right at the moment, the phone rang. I jumped up and swung around. I almost knocked Janet out of her chair, but I grabbed her to keep her from falling over. The phone rang again. We both hurried into the front room and stood over the ringing menace. I hesitated and then reached for the headset.

I shouted into the phone, "What?" There was a pause. A familiar voice spoke up.

"Where the hell have you two been? My man lost you after you got on that buggy. You were told not to leave the city and now you're back. Do I need to remind you, you're still under investigation? Do I have to haul your asses in and keep you locked up? You may have some pretty important friends, but I'll guarantee you one thing Mr..."

bzzzzzzzzzzzzzz the phone died. A loud crackle like a static charge liked to have knocked the phone out of my hand. I said into the phone, "Hello, hello?"

"Sorry for that unfortunate reprobate's harangue, David." It was Ce. "I'll have him chastised for his manners," he continued.

I told him it didn't matter. I didn't pay much attention to what he was saying anyway. I don't know why, but in my mindset at that time, I felt numb and couldn't care less about anything.

Ce coughed a little wheezing cough and said, "I'm sorry for your distress, but you must understand that there is evil in this world that moves between the spectrum of light and good. It hides in a shadowy doorway or in the glare from the noon sun; weak, but still evil enough to steal into a man's soul and naught at a man's eternity. What I had to show you, hurt me deeply. You were at a crossroads at that point. The good in you fighting the battle against the evil of men and hell; the evil in you swelling, pushing against the reason that separates you from the chaos of the hell bound. When Jesus was being questioned at one point in the Bible, was he not accused by some fool that he was a demon? If you remember his comment to that was, 'a house divided cannot stand.' Evil thrives on chaos. It is the worm that eats its own tail. It thrives on its division. You, old son, are caught in the yen and yang of this un-reality. It is my duty to our families and the friendship I shared with your father to keep you from being thrown into the 'fiery pits of perdition.' So, listen to the rest of what I have to tell you about your father. Stay indoors. If you need anything, Snid will get it for you. By the way, the two men that were left in my keeping will not bother mankind again. They attempted an escape from Snid. Unfortunately, their survival skills were not up to the swamp's aggressive nature. I need not say more on the subject".

The phone clicked and the familiar buzzing tone filled my ear. During Ce's conversation, Janet had been standing by me and I had positioned the phone so she could hear what he would say. We both looked at the TV and the couch. Then, we both sighed in unison. We both wanted this to end. The sooner we heard "the rest of the story," we hopefully could get the hell out of Louisiana and back to Memphis where the only thing we had to worry about was the standard stuff like crooked government, raciest cops, potholes, interstate construction, and an ever burgeoning crime rate.

I took the coffee pot and filled the mugs. The cinnamon rolls had glazed over again, but *what the hey*. Janet got her pen and the pad. Positioning ourselves on the couch, I hit the remote buttons and the whirr of the V.C.R.s and audible static from the TV filled the void. The first thing we saw was Ce hanging up the phone. My gut rolled and I squeezed Janet's hand while she squeezed me back. How was he doing this crap??????

He sat in the old chair. Snid's shadow floated around in the background and finally settled. I noticed a new piece of hardware on the back wall, the JuJu staff. I pointed it out to Janet and she shivered. Ce rolled his head back and the whites of his already white eyes shown like dead gray pearls. He began to speak.

Dick woke amid some words in his drowsy mind saying to him, "Sleeping is a reconciling, A rest that peace begets..." He shook his head and the smell of the coal oil lamp filled his lungs causing him to sputter a little. He slung his legs off the cot and stood up, then stretched. Joints popped and he growled like a bear coming out of hibernation. He'd had a good sleep. He rubbed his eyes, snorted, and spit a hocker onto the rock floor. Hunger pangs rolled over him. He looked at the shelf and saw he was down to one can of beans and a can of cling peaches. Grabbing the beans, Dick decided to make the most of his situation and share the odiferous nature of the aftermath of the beans with the world around him and save the peaches for his evening meal. He cut the can open and began to devour the contents. As he inhaled large bites quickly, his mind began to figure out ways he could make enough money to live on his own and still help his mother.

He thought about the fresh game he could sell at the meat cutters and the fish of course, but he knew the real money was in being a sugar boy for the men who made the "shine." He had always hated the thought of these men. Their shine had helped cause the riff between his father and him. It had caused his mother, indirectly, to be a slave to what was left of his father and after what happened between his father and him, what the hell. Better to deal with a devil you know. Right? Dick's plan was to head into town and make these men give him a job, come hell or high water. He'd be in tall cotton making the money he heard these men shelled out to the sugar boys that worked for them. Once his plan was laid out, he did not hesitate.

Dick scurried from the hole and made his way toward the environs of Nolensville proper. He wasn't quite sure if the sheriff would lay into him or not when other people were around for support and security. One on one, Dick knew the sheriff would piss his pants if they tangled again, or put a bullet in Dick.

When he arrived on the outskirts of town, Dick made his way around carefully. He stopped at the meat cutters and made arrangements for getting the fresh game to them. His next stop was the general store, better known as the five and dime. Dick shimmied up the rain gutter pipe at the back of the store and scooted across the low roof. The large storefront was false and Dick maneuvered through the support beams like a spider on a web. He and Bad Eye would come to the roof sometimes and watch the pedestrians and traffic move about the small city. Today though, Dick was looking for tell tale signs that people of official nature were looking for him. One thing he didn't want to do was bring any attention to the "five" who ran all the "shining" in this area.

Dick surveyed the street in front of the store including as many vehicles and people as he could, to ascertain if anyone or anything was not right. For a young man, he had a sense of regularity about territories. All living things were animals to an extent and all animals have territorial regularities, as he put it. He had watched these two-legged animals mark their territories just as craftily as the wood folk did. He saw the trucks and wagons of the vendors and the townfolks' cars he knew. The odd car or truck was an indication of tourists, visitors, and possibly a revenuer. Dick's scan of the area found the "odd man out," as it were. The car sat at the corner of Wilkes and Stratford with a hard view of the front door of the store. A man could sit there and watch the goings and comings of anyone visiting the store and from that perch, not be considered a source of inquiry. Dick made an effort to memorize the plate number on the car.

He retraced his steps and shimmied down the gutter pipe again. There was a crawl space at the end of the building where, on occasion, he and Bad Eye would sneak in under the flooring and listen to the conversations of the numerous people that frequented the store. At one spot, there was a trap door that lead to the back storeroom. The locked entrance to the crawl space was an effort by the store's owner to keep some of the more enterprising drunks that sometimes "slept it off" in the alley, from crawling under the building and accidentally setting the building on fire trying to light a smoke when they passed out.

Dick looked at the lock. It was the same one that was always there. He pulled the toothpick from his pocket and put the point into a small hole in the bottom of the lock. The lock opened as smoothly as a deacon's mouth eating chicken. Dick got to his knees and moved forward into the dark opening. After he was all the way in, he scooted around and fastened the small door back to its locked position. One of the boards would come undone if enough force was put on it. If a person knew the who's and what ifs of the door, they could be in and no one would be the wiser. And, Dick was in the know.

He walked on his knees and made a beeline to the trap door. He heard the murmurings of the people above him, but paid it little heed. When he got to the trap door, he positioned himself under it and sat for a moment. He bent his head to his chest and took a deep breath. All the sounds of the world faded as he exhaled. Then, as if he were in the woods, he cocked an ear to the surface world and cataloged each sound he heard. He did this for approximately a minute, then he was up through the floor like a gin from a magic lamp. Moving over to the pickle barrels and hunkering down so he wouldn't be seen by a clerk looking for an item a customer wanted, Dick waited again. He managed to secure a somewhat comfortable position and leaned back against the barrel. The brine and vinegar smell from the pickles made him hungry. He closed his eyes and let the sounds of the store fill his ears.

Dick heard the radio playing old time country songs. He heard a woman asking questions about a bolt of material she wanted to buy. He heard snatches of a dozen conversations and finally honed in on the "five." They usually sat near the oversized potbelly stove in the right rear of the store. An area was set aside for these "patrons" so they would have a place to congregate while their "cooking" was chugging away in some hidden hollow out in the then "wooded" areas around the county's perimeters.

The five seemed to be just a bunch of "old boys" who liked to play checkers and tell each other tall tales. In reality, it was a complex business meeting for the making and distributing of their product. Dick understood that all of this was clandestine. These seemingly "country bumpkins" were smart and had kept the government at bay for many years with their network of suppliers and runners. One of the smartest things they did was to avoid being around any of the stills. They hired "shiners" to do the actual work and they reaped the profits. Now, these old boys probably would look at someone throwing out words like supply and demand, bottom line, quality assurance, and quality control as a little strange. They worked on time-tested methods for making the "serum" and trusted the men who made it for them. They also tasted the finished product before it left the confines of the hollows. Anyone making substandard "mash" would be severely bashed and have their reputation smeared. With the money they made, this rarely ever happened. As for Dick, he just wanted enough money to keep his mother happy and to keep his life as a fisherman and a hunter going. If trucking with the devil was the way to do this, then he'd set his mind to get it done.

He opened his eyes and began to watch the door that lead to the store proper. He saw a woman with four children walk past and that was all he needed to affect his entrance into the retail world surrounding him. He hurried to the door and saw one of the children hanging back. The woman spoke out loud and told all of her children to stay close. At that, Dick popped out of the storage room and joined the other children for a second, then he began to maneuver through the isles toward the "five." The closer he got, the louder they seemed to talk. He stopped next to a rack of hoes and took a deep breath. On exhaling, he sauntered over to the "five" and stood before them. They all stopped in mid-sentence and stared a hole in him.

Mr. Greg, the head of the group, spoke up and growled, "What the hell do you want, boy?"

Dick swallowed hard and looked Mr. Greg in the eye, then said, "I want to be a 'sugar boy'."

Mr. Greg looked at him with disgust and impunity. Then, he laughed and when he did, so did the others. Dick turned red and almost ran from the store, but he caught himself and stood there.

"What's a 'sugar boy', boy? We don't have tits to sugar, so we don't need no 'sugar boy.'"

Dick stayed still. His hand instinctively went to the pocket that held his toothpick and his other hand moved toward his old handmade knife.

"What you doing, boy? You gettin' ready to wipe the snot from your nose?"

Mr. Billy made this comment. The group laughed in unison again and that really pissed Dick off. Holding on to his blades, Dick took off running toward the table the group sat around. He let out a blood curdling scream, jumped up flat-footed and landed on top of the table with his two "stickers" in hand. This took the old boys totally by surprise and Mr. Cliff and J.C. fell backwards out of their chairs. The toothpick was an inch away from old Mr. Franklin's throat. A tense silence filled the area around the table. Mr. Franklin sat there bug-eyed and quiet. Dick took a look around the store. Almost every- one in town knew that part of the store was off limits to civilians and officers of the law. If you did by chance, trespass into the sanctum of the "five", depending on the mood of the boys on any given day, you'd hear enough about your animal ancestry and questionable legitimacy to darn well make sure you'd never make that mistake again.

Dick spoke up and said, "Don't give me any shit, you pecker woods, or I'll cut this old boy from gullet to asshole and sing a tune doing it."

Mr. Franklin broke his silence at that. In a somewhat sheepish voice, he muttered, "What tune would that be, little son?"

Dick still kept the toothpick close to Franklin's throat and brandished his old handmade blade toward the others. Dick slowly turned to Mr. Franklin.

Looking him in the eye he said loudly so all the others could hear, "My daddy chews tobacco, my momma dips her snuff, and if you ask'em 'bout me, they'll tell you straight, old Dick, he don't do nothin', 'cause he's tough enough."

A big smile came over Mr. Franklin's face while Mr. Greg snickered and at that, all the "five" guffawed. After they had their laugh, the "five" told Dick to put his blades away. They'd talk to him about a job. Dick hung on a minute, then stood up. He jumped from the table and kept his blades at the ready. Mr. Franklin rubbed his neck and looked for blood only to find transudation.

He spoke up and said, "Okay, Dick, if that's your name. Put the blades up, you're in."

Dick hesitated, shrugged, then slid the knives into their respective pockets. Standing there now unarmed, he was somewhat less formidable in his demeanor.

"Alright, boy," Mr. Greg said, "Who are you and how do you know about our business?"

"My name's Dick, Dick Madison." At the mention of his last name the "five" all turned and looked at him.

"You any kin to the Madisons that live out near Flat Rock?" asked Mr. Cliff.

"Yes sir, he's my grandfather." Dick said. The "five" all shook their heads in unison at that bit of news.

"So, you're old Madison's grandboy," said Mr. Greg. "Well, you got quite a reputation around town, son. We understand you left the sheriff in a pickle awhile ago".

Dick flushed at that. He didn't think the sheriff would have spread that incident around. But then he figured it was like his mama told him, little town, big ears.

"And you're part Indian and mountain man, we understand. You know the woods around here pretty well."

"Yes sir, I do know the woods and the rivers and creeks from these parts down to Nashville and up to Murfreesboro and around. I plan to know more."

"You will boy, you will." The others nodded yes, too. Mr. Greg told Dick to be at "potato peel'en" road at daybreak the next day and they'd give him a tryout. Dick stood there a minute and shook his head in compliance.

"Okay, but first I need some money to buy some food. Then, I can start for you tomorrow."

The "five" looked at each other in utter bewilderment at that comment.

Mr. Cliff spoke up and said, "Boy, don't push your luck. You better get gone."

Dick spoke up again. "Give me some money, take it from my first pay, but I need to buy some food."

Mr. Billy stood up and started toward Dick. He was a big man and when he stood over Dick, it seemed Dick's head came to Mr. Billy's knees. Dick waited until the big man was about to run him down, then he fell forward and scrambled through the man's open legs. Before Mr. Billy could turn, Dick kicked him behind his right knee and the giant fell. He almost squashed Dick he fell so fast, but he slid out of the way, then was on him like stink on a stick.

"I told ya'll not to give me any shit." The toothpick sang in the air when Dick unleashed it. "All I want is a few bucks to tide me over. Take it out of my first pay."

"Okay, boy. Back on off, Billy," said Mr. Greg. "Here's five dollars."

Mr. Greg threw the wadded up bill at Dick. He caught it and stuffed it in his pocket. Then, he hopped up from the hold he had on old Billy and backed away. Keeping an eye out, he stopped at the front counter and bought a dozen cans of beans, some matches, a coke from the icebox, and a hunting magazine. After he paid for the things he'd wanted, he still had $3.50. He told the clerk to put all his stuff in a tote sack. He gave the store the once over again and then he left.

The "five" sat silent for a few minutes after helping Billy back to his seat. He murmured something about getting that "little bastard." Mr. Greg told Billy to leave Dick alone. The boy was a Madison, and by rights, he should be in the business. Anyway, they needed a new "sugar boy." Keeping new blood in the stock kept the "revenuers" running around like chickens. They all agreed with this assessment. Billy kept quiet, but marked Dick for payback.

Dick made his way through the town and back into the woods. Taking familiar trails, he was soon back at the "hole." Before he went in, he stopped at a nearby bluff and scraped out the old bugs and debris from the mouth of the small, cold spring that seeped from the rock formation. He gently laid the coke in the sand and the cold water flowed over the bottle. He'd come back for it right before he retired for the night and sip his treat while he read his magazine. He then darted into the confines of the hole.

Dick put the can goods and the matches in their assigned places. He folded the rough tote sack and placed it on the small bed like a pillow. He pulled out the money he had and took two dollars, and then put it back in his pocket. The other dollar and a half he put into the old cigar box he used to keep his money. He sequestered the box and gave the room the "everything has a place" look. Then, he popped up out of the hole and set off toward his momma's. In his mind, he saw her smile at him and hug him when he gave her the two dollars. She may even give him a fried pie for doing what she asked of him.

Dick got close to the house. The sun was beginning to recede behind the hills to the west and the light that was left made long shadows fall. He waited at the edge of the wood until he saw the kitchen light come on. Then, he slipped from the woods and slid along the back of the house. He perked up his ears to listen for signs that his father may have been there. All he heard was the familiar sound of pans and the puffing of the old stove being set up for cooking. He stole up the back steps and "kilroy'ed" over the window ledge.

As he peered in, he saw the back of his mother as she moved around the kitchen and he pssst at her. She turned around and looked at the place she thought the sound had come from. Dick saw a bruised eye and jaw and the rage welled up in him. He held it back though.

Bessie said out loud, "Dick, is that you? Come out where I can see you. Your father's not here yet."

At that, Dick stood up fully and opened the back door. Bessie didn't run to him as he'd hoped. She stood there wringing the old hand towel she always had with her in the kitchen. Dick pulled out the two dollars and handed it to her. She in turn, put the money in her apron pocket. No smile, no hug, nothing.

"Will you bring more the next time you come? I need to get a new frock."

Dick stood there. He saw his mother and he saw her greed. He knew then what his purpose was. *Feed the greed.*

He spoke up and said, "I start a job tomorrow. I will be running sugar for the boys at the store."

At that, his momma perked up. "Okay, son. I'll see you again on payday. You'd better get gone He'll' be home in a minute."

For Dick, the moment was as empty as air. No feelings passed from his mother in any way. He was just a means for her to get money. He raised his right hand toward her, then dropped it to his side. His head hung so low. His shoulders drooped to a point his knuckles could have dragged the floor and he could have kicked himself in the face when he walked.

He turned and left the kitchen the same way he came in and eventually, he found himself at the edge of the river that passed near the hole. The half moon and the stars reflected off the still water. Dick picked up a small rock and tossed it into the river. The splash broke the silence of his somber mood and the sounds of the night flooded into his waking mind. He stood there a minute longer and then he shook like a dog coming from an unwanted bath. He shook off all the feelings he had for his mother, the soft feelings. He replaced them with reality. Hard, cold, singular.

Running headstrong with this new realization, Dick got back to the hole. Lighting the lamp, the small space flooded with light. He pulled a can of beans from the fresh stocked shelf and opened it. He had forgotten about the coke, but as soon as he smelled the beans, he remembered it. He retrieved it from its resting place, colder than it had been in the store's icebox. He grabbed his new magazine and while he ate, he looked at all the new fangled items the advertisements showed and his mind cleared even more. He finished his beans, drank his coke, and closed his magazine. Stretching, he blew out the lamp. He then went to the cot and fluffed his new pillow.

He started a new life tomorrow. His mind was clear; he knew what he was going to do. He lay down and as sleep washed over him, he told himself that he was hard, he was steel, he needed nothing from anybody but money and he'd get that from working. He'd get it now by being a "sugar boy." Then, he'd learn how to make shine and start his own business. These thoughts finally dissolved into the blankness of sleep. Sometimes when a body needs to sleep sound, the mind sees it different and rolls for hours leaving one in a state of flux. The body responds by being worn-out and the mind becomes as lucent as a bowl of mush. This night though, Dick slept the sleep of the contented. The next morning his internal clock rang and he was up and out of the hole like a shot.

Chapter Twelve

Dick made his way through the dew covered woods to the meeting place where he'd be teamed up with a "sugar" that was familiar with the ways and means to do the job. After a trial period of a day or two, the "sugar" would give them his assessment of the new boy and the new kid would be employed or sent away with a few bucks in his pocket for his trouble. They would set a new meeting place and the process would start again.

As he approached the meeting place, Dick walked to the back of the wagon and watched the boy who would be his mentor for the next few days. The boy stood at the far end near the horses. Most of the boys Dick had seen were young, anywhere between his age and 15 years old. This kid looked every bit of 17 or18 years old. There was something about the boy that struck Dick with a recollection. He concentrated on the boy's face and then it dawned on him who the boy reminded him of, Mr. Billy from the store. This was old Billy's son.

Dick slid around to the other side of the wagon and kept his eyes peeled as he moved out of the boy's vision. He moved to the wood around the meeting place and got behind the "sugar." To Dick, blood was thicker than shit and the boy might want to see if he could do what his old man hadn't. Dick checked himself for his knives. A quick pat and he was ready to tangle with this comer, too. Feeling ready to handle whatever happened, Dick stepped from the woods and hurriedly walked up behind the "sugar." If the boy swung on Dick, he'd be hard pressed to do any damage to Dick as close in as Dick had placed himself.

"Hey, wet this morn'in, aint it."

The boy jumped into the air and jerked the reigns he was holding so hard the horses reared and almost started to run. Dick grabbed the leather from the boys grasp and pulled down on the reigns. The horses had that wide-eyed terror look horses get when they become frightened. Dick reached up to the horse right in front of him and started rubbing its nose and speaking softly to the animal. The other horse took note and it too, started to settle down. Dick began to alternate between the two and within moments, he had the team nuzzling him. Dick watched the "sugar" out of the corner of his eye while he tended the horses and saw the boy sitting on the ground. He spoke over his shoulder to the boy.

"You alright back there?"

The boy looked at Dick and then stood up. With both of his fists balled for punching, he shouted at Dick, "What in the hell do you think you're doing, boy? You've scared me out of a foot to grow and a year to live. I ought to beat your ass for comin' up on me like that."

Dick took the reigns and tied them to a limb from a bush next to the horse's heads. He turned and as he made the circle, he drew both his blades. The bright rays from the morning sun that slipped through the treetops glinted off the shining blade of the toothpick.

"Whoa, now boy, there's no need for cut'n me. I'm just scared. When I get scared, I shoot my mouth off. Please, don't hurt me."

Dick saw the shudder of fear pass through the older boy like watching a ripple in water. He put his blades aside, but kept them handy, just in case "shaky" was trying to pull something.

"My name is Dick," he said loudly. "Who are you?"

"My name is John. "My daddy is…"

"I know who your daddy is," interrupted Dick. "He and I tangled last night at the store." John's face flushed red and he looked as if he was trying to control himself.

"I know," he said. "My daddy was so mad when he got home last night, he couldn't see straight He almost kissed the dog and put momma outside."

This statement threw Dick for a minute. When he gained his composure, he caterwauled with laughter. John came out with a small laugh. Dick walked up to him and extended his hand. John looked at Dick and Dick's hand like they were from another world. John, still hesitating, met Dick's hand with his and they shook. To Dick, shaking hands with John was like shaking an old rag. A few minutes later, they were ready to head into town to pick up a load of sugar. Getting up on the wagon, John handed Dick the reigns.

On the way in, John started talking ninety miles an hour. Dick listened and nodded every now and again, but his main concentration was his surroundings. Dick knew that if he were going to do this job, he needed to get in and out of town with as little fuss as possible to keep the "John Law" off his trail. He had come into town this way sometimes with his momma when she had to run errands. Too many people. Too much traffic. Dick had a dozen ways in and out of the town without too much fanfare. If this old wagon was going to be his or one like it, he'd be in and out before any of the everyday townies could spit.

The tape shut off, the phone rang, and there was someone knocking at the door. I almost jumped out of my skin and off the couch. Janet stood up so fast, she dropped all her writing materials on the floor. We panicked for a second, then we moved. I almost knocked her down heading for the door while she went to the phone. I stopped at the door and looked at Janet. She was at the phone. She went to pick up the receiver and I opened the door. When I swung it open, I saw Hobart and two uniformed officers. At the same time, I heard Janet say "okay" over and over. I looked at Hobart and shook my head.

"What now?' I asked. Hobart had a folded piece of paper in his hand and he handed it to me.

"I got a warrant this time, slick," he intoned pushing past me with the uniforms in tow.

"What the hell have we allegedly done now?"

"Two bodies were found, dumped, deposited, whatever, at the precinct. They had been, let me put this delicately, torn all to hell. The guts and the whole abdominal cavity were gone just like the stiff we found at the morgue. You remember the morgue, don't you?"

Janet said one more okay and put the receiver slowly back in the cradle. She stood there for a moment and shook her head like she was trying to get rid of, or shake something into her brain. I had a guess in my mind that it was Ce or Snid on the other end of the phone and Janet was given some information that may be useful in this situation. On the other hand, maybe it was just more of his crap. I didn't know anything at this point, except I was being smart-mouthed by some dickhead cop. Janet came toward me. One of the cops stopped her. I took a step toward them and Hobart pulled his piece and took a defensive stance. I stopped dead cold. "Hold it right there, buckaroo One more step and I'll have to do a lot of paperwork in the morning and I'm not in the mood."

"Okay, so why are you bringing warrants to hassle us? What do you expect us to do about it?"

"One of the 'victims' had a water bottle stuck in the regions where the sun don't shine. We dusted it for prints, and guess what? Your prints were all over the thing. We also had a test done on the liquid traces inside the bottle and found a heavy concentration of 'sage.' I thought that was funny because these birds didn't have any stuffing to speak of."

"Let me see, you found a bottle with some sage in

it up somebody's ass and my fingerprints were all over the bottle. After all that has happened to me and Janet since we've been here, why in hell are you still busting my balls? The bottle was obviously planted. I can't figure what the 'sage' has to do with anything."

"Well," said Hobart, "it seems, according to the lab people and DEA, 'sage' is a drug coming up from south of the border. It's hallucinogenic and addictive. Because it's distilled from the common herbal sage plant, our government hasn't deemed it illegal as yet. Its natural elements make it a bad one to use or slip to others. Why did you put it in a water bottle?"

I was listening to Hobart prattle on and feigning that I was paying attention, but mostly I was trying to figure out how to cover our collective ass. When he spat out the "why did you put it ..." A light went off in my head and I jumped at the chance to come back with a "what the hell do you mean by that?" He formed a half smile and realized I'd caught on to his ruse.

"Just checking," he said. I wanted to grab my crank like the guys in the movies do and yell, "Check this!" but I didn't. I just tried to stare a hole through him.

Hobart gave the cop who was keeping Janet away from me a nod and he backed off. She moved toward me making short steps. When she finally got close enough to whisper, she told me she did this to keep the cops, especially Hobart, from saying she had made "a sudden move" and pop a cap in her. I reached down and gently kissed her on the forehead. She whispered to me that Ce had been the caller and told her that something would happen soon and Hobart and his "happy boys" would be called away. I just nodded at her.

Before I got my head to stop moving, Hobart's radio let out with a garbled squelched request that pissed old flatfoot off to the point he kicked a small trash can nearby with a vengeance. It flew into the cop that had been holding Janet putting a nice little cut in his chin. This infuriated Hobart even more and he was cussing so much, I put my hands over Janet's ears. She blushed and this set him off again.

"Okay people, stand down. Everybody out."

Hobart glared at us with what I consider, pure hate. He holstered his gun and walked up to me. Standing flat-footed he looked into my face and his eyes darted around as though he were trying to find some entrance into my head. A minute passed and neither he nor I said anything to each other. He stopped his staring game and just shook his head, turned, and left the room. No goodbye, no sorry, nada. I took my hands off Janet's ears and gently held her face for a second, then I smiled and gave her a kiss. She responded, nicely.

We were embraced when the front door slammed shut. We both jumped. I pushed her down to the couch and had my Buck ready for whatever. As it grew silent again, the phone rang. I hesitated; Janet grabbed the receiver. She looked at me and I held out my hand for her to give me the phone. She started to hand it to me and put her free hand over the mouthpiece.

"Be nice." It was Hobart.

"Look I don't know how you've wrangled out of this and I don't give a shit, but let me tell you this, boy. If you so much as whistle the wrong tune, I'm going to nail you! Don't leave town."

I thought he was hanging up on his end. There was sudden quiet, but for some reason, I noticed there was no phone noise, like the usual silence, then the abrupt "clicking" when the phone is set in the cradle. The next thing I heard were the sounds like a phone being passed around or handled without the handler paying attention to what's going on. I looked at Janet with my "What the Fu---

--" look, then I heard, "David". It was unmistakably, Ce. "Forgive Officer Hobart's over zealousness, He's like a tic sometimes. When he gets his head into what he thinks is a big dog, or in this scenario a 'big case,' he won't let it go until he's full and satisfied that he's done all he can. I know these constant interruptions are causing you and Janet cabin fever. I'm going to give you a few days to unwind and enjoy the city. Let me caution you though, always be watchful. There is evil present at all times." A long pause ensued.

Abruptly Ce spoke again, "During the day I suggest you do the 'Riverwalk' and take a tour or two. During the evening hours, I suggest you try a blend of the culinary delights we here in Na'lens are proud of. If I may be so bold, I would suggest tonight you have dinner at 'Mr. B's' pasta jambalaya, magnifique! Tomorrow night, I suggest 'Emril's.' The menu is vast and the wine list is fabulous. I think you will enjoy the services of a waiter by the name of Alexander. On the third evening, you must seek out the repast at 'Sbisa' near the Market. There the ambiance will put you in the mood for sumptuous delights and perhaps... ask for Tom to be your server. There is a presence at Sbisa's on the third floor. The area is closed to the public, but on occasion a private tour is arranged. Perhaps you will feel the presence and remember a *yesterday* of your father. In all the places I've mentioned, use my name. We will start our business again in a few days. Snid will let you know. 'In medias res' as it's said."

Bzzzzzzzzzzzzzzzz the phone could only utter this sound and the voice stopped as suddenly as it intervened.

I hung the handset back into the cradle and looked at Janet's pensive face, then I sat beside her on the couch. I was still trying to come to a reality check. Janet put the squeeze on my arm and I instinctively gave her a kiss. I closed my eyes for a second, took a deep breath, and smiled

a big "Cheshire" cat grin. She poked me with a What? I
started telling her what Ce had just related to me and her
face beamed with anticipation. She and I both looked at our
watches at the same time. It was about 6:30 p.m.

Janet grabbed the phone book and looked up the
restaurant Ce had mentioned we should go to that evening,
"Mr. B's". She reached for the phone and dialed the
number.

"Hello, I would like to make reservations for
tonight..." Janet looked up at me. She was frowning. I
motioned for her to put her hand over the phone and then I
mouthed her to tell them Mr. Stringfellow suggested them.
Janet looked puzzled for a second. She spoke up to the
person on the other end and said, "Mr. Stringfellow
suggested we visit your restaurant, but if......you have a
table?... Tonight, 9:00p.m., Madison, for two." Janet recited
the phone number for the condo, ended with a thank you
and hung up the phone.

"Yes!" she shouted, "We're out of here."

She stood up and a look of horror fell across her
face.

I grabbed her and shouted, "What's wrong?"

She looked at me and said, "I don't have anything
to wear."

I let go of her and sat back down on the couch. My
heart was still beating faster than I liked, but I managed a
giggle.

I looked at her and said, "Let's go shopping."

For some reason, I picked up the remotes for the
video player and the TV. A feeling of dread passed through
my spine, and I dropped the remotes as though I'd been
shot. Janet put her hands on my shoulders and whispered to
me to let go. I patted her left hand and stood up and took
her other hand. We went to the bedroom and got dressed.

From our condo, the River Walk was only seven

blocks. We made it without any incidents. Daylight in that part of the city shades the dirt enough to give the tourist a plastic view of reality. As we arrived at the River Walk, we had a few hours free so we opted for a riverboat cruise. The ride was comforting and relaxing. The captain pointed out items of interest, I guess. I tried to keep a watchful eye out for the "evil" old Ce spoke of. Janet was delighted to be in the sun and for some reason the day was not as sweltering as we had encountered in our other excursions.

When we docked, Janet said she was a tad hungry and I was parched. I figured we'd grab something in the food court. Talk about your choices, the place was one big choice. We decided to grab a gyro and a coke. Then we decided to shop till we dropped.

The shops were varied. Everything from hats to stores that sold "gatortail" snacks. There were a few kiosks that sold shirts and knickknacks. One kiosk we stopped at was selling raffle tickets to win a trip to Italy, 10 days in Rome, all expenses paid. I hesitated but the, "please" look I got from Janet broke me down and I sprung for a ticket. The hawker said the funds would go to help the schools in the outlying areas of Louisiana Yeah, right. I folded the stub I was suppose to keep, but Janet secured it in her purse. Away we went.

We shopped and Janet found a nice black dress with a net-looking shawl. Then, she picked me out a tie and a few other things she wanted us to wear for our other evenings out and about.

We left the River Walk and decided to stroll back to the condo. The walk back was uneventful. I felt an odd sense of being watched, but I couldn't put a face with the watcher and left it alone. I didn't say anything to Janet, but I made damn sure I had access to my "little friends."

Janet was a knockout in the new clothes and I can say with pride I didn't look too shabby either. We walked around to the area where Mr. B's was located and mingled with the crowd of tourists. Around 8:30 p.m., we decided to have a drink. We went into Mr. B's and headed toward the bar where I found a couple of seats. The bartender asked for our preferences. I ordered a vodka and cranberry with a twist of lime for Janet. I saw they had Buckler and ordered one of those for myself. Janet was ecstatic. She was enjoying a day and night of not having to look over her shoulder or get writer's cramps. I too, was in a lively mood. Somewhere in the back of my mind, I could still hear Ce telling me to watch out for the "evil" that can swoop in showing up at the most inopportune times. My mood was light, but I watched as cautioned. Somewhere in the Bible it says that God respects no man. After all the nonsense we had been through, I was beginning to agree with that concept whole-heartedly.

At the assigned hour, I walked up to the hostess and told her we had reservations. Janet had walked downstairs to the lady's room to freshen up. I told the hostess my name and she looked on her list. She hesitated. I stood there smiling at her. She motioned to a man near the kitchen and he came over to where we were. The hostess whispered something in his ear and he looked at me. He took two menus from the table situated at the hostess' podium and said, "Follow me." Janet came up behind me at that moment and I motioned for her to move ahead of me and follow the man with the menus. We wound our way through the restaurant to a flight of stairs. The man with the menus stopped, turned, and pointed up. A small balcony overlooked the whole restaurant and that, it seemed, would be our sanctuary.

Janet and I went up the stairs and behind us came the menu man. There was a small table overlooking the dining area and front door. A settee and a coffee table were against the wall behind us with a couple of overstuffed chairs facing the settee. "Menu man" pulled Janet's chair out for her. We sat down at the table. Before I could adjust my chair, Menu man snapped his fingers and a waiter appeared from the shadows with a bottle of champagne. "Compliments of Mr. Stringfellow," he said.

Janet's eyes sparkled and I was a Cheshire cat with the smile I gave. Menu man bowed and disappeared down the stairs.

Our waiter came to the table and asked if he could, at our convenience, recite the specials of the day. I nodded my approval and he intoned a large list of yummies. We settled for the "Pasta Jambalaya" for our main course, ordering salads and hot bread before the meal. Overlooking the dining area, the sounds of laughter and enjoyment filtered up to us and we smiled while Janet drank the wine Ce had sent and I stayed with my Buckler. This was going to be a good night and we were finally enjoying the Na'lens we had heard so much about.

We spent the evening moving back and forth from the table to the couch. Cleansing our pallets with sherbet between courses and sipping coffee. After we left Mr. B's, we wandered aimlessly around the crowded streets like the other tourists and ended up back at the condo, tired puppies. There was no hesitation for sleep that night. Upon our usual Spooning, we were out like lights.

I awoke the next morning with a start as I sat straight up in bed. Janet, awakened by my movements, also sat up. We looked at each other and waited. Something woke us up. Janet held her finger to her lips for me not to say anything. I listened, cocking my head back and forth to pick up on any sound. After a few seconds of listening intently, it dawned on me. The silence. The silence is what woke me. No jackhammers, no street noise, no TV's, nothing. I flopped back in the bed and Janet snuggled up close to me. We still hadn't spoken. I kissed her on the top of her head, closed my eyes, and fell back to sleep.

Sometime near the 10 o'clock hour, we managed to crawl out of bed and start stretching. We hadn't slept so long since...well, I can't remember. I stumbled to the kitchen and cranked up the coffee. While I was trying to focus, I heard the shower start and found myself following the sound. I pulled back the shower curtain and was enveloped in the wonderful regenerative powers of the steamy water and Janet, the same. The rest of the morning is none of your business.

The rest of the daylight hours, Janet and I spent milling about the outlying malls and sight seeing. I hooked up with a guide for a few hours of swamp tours and we got back to the condo about twilight. We were famished and that night we had reservations at Emeril's.

After all the walking and slogging through swamps we had done during the day, we opted for a cab to take us to Emeril's. We were greeted upon entering the restaurant and asked about our reservations. I spoke the magic words, Ceolophus Stringfellow. Eyes lit up, people scurried, and presto changeo, a man in a suit had us follow him to a table. We were expecting something on the order of what we had at Mr. B's as far as the table setting and such, but no. We were taken to an area near the kitchen. I thought at first we were going to be seated in the area where the silverware was rolled into the napkins and have some person who was on break sitting next to us at a table with their shoes off complaining about being on their feet all day. I'm glad I don't say a lot of this shit out loud. "Mr. Suit" turned as we approached the entry to the kitchen and we were seated in an area where the man himself ate when he was at the restaurant. When we were settled at our table, Mr. Suit removed a reserved sign from it. The location in the restaurant was quiet and the lighting was adjusted to a pleasant level so we could see everything and enjoy being romantic in conducive atmosphere. I was relaxed finally.

Along the restaurant wall, I noticed thousands of corks, individual corks from bottles of wine. Names and dates were written on them showing to all, a badge of fame that states, "I have eaten here, and I am apart from the crowd." We were exited and couldn't wait to start. Within a moment of being seated, a young man appeared bringing water glasses and filled them for us. He told us our waiter would be "Alexander." He also asked if we wanted something from the bar. I asked for a wine list so I could pick out a wine for Janet before we ordered our meal and I wanted to see what non-alcoholic goodies were available for me. Ah! Buckler again for me and a nice, light Sauvignon Blanc for Janet.

I ordered a huge baked pork chop and steamed veggies. Janet had duck in an orange sauce. We ate until I had to drop a notch in my belt. I must say, being attended to by Alexander was a treat. He had the experience and intuition that made him highly professional in his work.

Again, two stuffed ducks waddled out of the restaurant. We agreed to walk off the sumptuous meal, so we decided to go to Harrah's and tease the slot monkeys. I ended up playing Caribbean poker. By 2 a.m., I added up the good, bad, and ugly and found myself even. Janet and I literally ran out of there, hopped in a cab, and headed back to the condo. We laughed all the way back, recounting the look on the dealer's face when I won the last hand and announced I'd had enough, got up, left him a five dollar chip, and took off.

When we got back to the condo, this time we didn't even make it to bed. Janet and I plopped down on the couch when we got inside. Later that morning, we found ourselves entwined and wrinkled. About 8 a.m., I woke up with the awareness that my right arm had pushed itself under the cushions and the circulation had all but stopped. I was face down on the couch. Somehow, Janet had managed to work her feet under the back of my coat. One foot was sticking out of the neck hole. I was glad no one was there with a camera. A few minutes of push and pull, grunt and squeal, found us emerging from our entanglement. We headed toward the bedroom leaving a trail of clothes behind us. Still sleepy, we both crawled into bed, spooned, and without much maneuvering, fell asleep again.

The next time I opened my eyes was 1 p.m. The afternoon sun had pushed its way through the mini blinds and filled the room in slices. If memory serves me, I think the average human moves about 32 times in the course of sleeping 8 hours. I think Janet and I went to the moon and back with all the contortions we created during sleep.

I stumbled over my pants heading toward the bathroom. It didn't have windows, so I flicked on the light. Holding onto the sink, my head down so the light wouldn't blow out my unfocused eyes, I breathed deeply and heard the squishy phlegm in my lungs rush toward my throat. One of the hazards of hanging out in casinos is filling my lungs with second hand smoke. After spitting out a big hocker of slime, I thought to myself how stupid it was for people to smoke and fuck up their bodies. Ah well, I thought... if anybody wanted my opinion, they'd slap it out of me. But I knew my opinion on smoking was popular.

I finally looked into the mirror and was about to scream from seeing the reflection, when it hit me. I was looking at myself. My long hair had come undone, and with the bags under my eyes, man, I could have scared the U off ugly. I heard Sweetness in the kitchen cranking up the coffee pot. Even though it was late, a day without caffeine is piss poor. I threw water on my old face and head, combed my hair, and brushed my nasty teeth.

Refreshed, I boldly headed for the smell of java. Entering the kitchen, I saw Janet sitting with her legs under her at the little table, head in her hands, and a half empty cup of coffee on the table by her elbow. I said, "Hey." She in turn said, "Gihhfhgehik." I took that to mean, "Hey, now shut up and leave me alone." I poured myself a cup of the magic brew and sat down at the table. I bravely let my right hand caress her arm closest to me. She didn't even flinch. Funny how too much sleep is worse than not enough sometimes. Janet dropped her hands, lifted the cup of coffee to her lips, and drank deeply.

Looking at me, she managed a snarly smile and said, "Shower." I just nodded in agreement. She abruptly stood up, put her arms out in front of her and walked to the bathroom. I heard the door shut, the shower turn on, and a heavy sigh of enjoyment.

We managed a halfhearted adventure of wandering around the market area the rest of the afternoon. We dropped by a store that made fresh pralines and sampled enough of the different kinds along with the coffee to get a sugar rush that lasted for hours. We steered clear of the voodoo stores and the vendors that sold all that bogus bull related to anything "unnatural." We went to the old mint and enjoyed the walking tour. All in all it was a relatively quiet and stress-free day.

Twilight was approaching and we decided to head back to the condo, change into some of our new clothes, and then, leisurely retrace our steps back to the market. Having only consumed coffee and sugar all day, by the time our reservations at "Sbisa" came along, I was ready to eat the old horse. We strolled down to the market and stopped a couple of times so Janet could look at the masks and trinkets she may not have seen during the day.

We arrived at "Sbisa's" on time for our reservations. I looked at the guest list and saw that our names were highlighted. When I told the host who we were, he began to pop out in a cold sweat along his forehead. For some reason, he rubbed his hands together, too. I gave him my "Well, what's your problem" look and he snapped out of whatever zone he had fallen into.

"Oh, yes, yes, the friends of Mr. Stringfellows!" I thought for a moment he was going to hug us.

Snatching two menus from the podium he was standing at, he turned and walked semi-backwards, trying to maintain a conversation with Janet and me.

"It's been awhile, I mean the last time Mr. Stringfellow was here. We do so enjoy his visits."

With that said, a "I'll just hush now" look fell on his face. The restaurant was filled with the assortment of tourists one always sees and are usually a part of. I assumed our host was going to seat us near a group from somewhere like "Clawhamer,Tennessee" or some smarmy well-to-dos from above the Mason Dixon line. I was hoping not to be surrounded by anyone, if possible. Periodically, our host would turn his head and look at us to be sure we were still following him.

We went all the way through the main floor dining area, past the kitchen, and outside into a courtyard. It was great. The foliage had little bright lights entwined among their branches. There were only two tables. The trickling stream from a small fountain flowed along the lower edge of the high wall to the back of the courtyard. Water ran into a pool where large Chinese goldfish swam beneath the dim reflections given off by the artificial light from the foliage and candles on the tables. A small figure of a young girl, partially hidden by the large leafs of an elephant ear plant, caught my eye. She seemed to be holding a bowl of some sort in her left hand and a long dagger in her right hand. The table where we were seated was just a few feet away.

I was just about to question our host about the seating arrangement when he let out a "dough boy" squeal and headed back the way we had come. I looked at Janet across the table and just shook my head a little.

"Leave it to Ce to inspire us on our last night of freedom."

When I said that, Janet said she was happy and this was an unusually romantic setting. I looked at her again and marveled at the way the lights accented her beauty. It was like the pale light was gathering around something softer than itself and protecting her from the harshness of the real world. The atmosphere emphasized the knockout my wife really was.

The courtyard held a smell of earth and moisture, an old garden smell. The smell of fresh turned earth from a new grave was an odd description that popped in my mind. It was a faint smell, but it was there. I was getting pissed at myself for getting into that kind of mood and focused on Janet together with our night out to push the morbid thoughts out of my head. I was hoping a waiter or someone would come and bust the brain fart I was having. I guess I pleaded my case in my head strongly enough, that something picked up on it.

I heard the footfalls of someone coming to the table. I turned to see a man walking with a peculiar gate, ambling to the table. He stood there a second, as if eyeing some sort of prey, and trying to figure out which one to eat first. Janet looked up at him and a sudden change of facial expression enveloped his countenance. It looked to me to be an expression of reverence, a beauty and beast thing. I spoke then and asked him for a wine list and some water for Janet and myself. For the response I received, I could have given my request to the statue behind the plants. Janet saw my "flames" begin to edge up around my neck and quickly said to our visitor, "Please". He immediately gave her a short bow and walked away toward the main dining area. It took no more than one or two minutes at the most for our server to return with the items I had requested.

He was very official upon his return to the table. He set our glasses up and poured the water from a silver pitcher. I watched his hands as he maneuvered the glasses and water pitcher. On his left hand was a ring of what appeared to be black onyx. It was a long ring for a man to wear. When he bent his finger at the joint, the ring set forward in the space. At the time, I thought I saw the shape of something move within the ring. I was going to ask him about it when the shape disappeared as the lighting changed with his movement. It was as though whatever it was within the gem dove deeper into the blackness of the stone. Then, after putting the pitcher down, he snapped open the wine list. The sound of the snap reverberated off the bricks that enclosed the courtyard. The sound startled Janet and she jumped a little in her seat. Our server spoke. His voice was soothing to the ear, a tone not unlike the tones found in the calming effect of organ music.

"Pardon me madam, I apologize for the rudeness of my action. Normally, there are enough people coming and going here to act as a ballast for the sounds, but since it is just you and Mr. Madison..." At that I perked up and listened somewhat more closely. "My name is Tom," he said, "and I will be your waiter and your guide tonight. Mr. Stringfellow has asked me personally to protect. . . , excuse me, see to your comforts and enjoyment this evening."

A red flag went up in my head when I caught the "protect...." part of his spiel. I wanted to find out what that slip of the tongue was really about; but to do so, would probably upset Janet and the evening so, I just sat there and smiled. He suggested a white wine to Janet. Before we ordered, Tom snapped his fingers and as if out of nowhere came another person caring a Buckler on a tray along with Janet's wine. Her eyes had a gleeful "isn't this grand" look and I melted into her happiness. Tom asked if we would like a few minutes to look over the menus. I said that I would like for him to suggest the evening's repast; from soup, salad, main entree, and dessert. Janet shook her head to signify agreement. Tom smiled.

It was either the lighting or the angle of his head because when his mouth opened and exposed his teeth, he displayed large canines similar to the ones I saw protruding from Ce's mouth the night we first met him. I did one of my "oh shits" in my head and dropped my hand down to find "old Buck." Tom never skipped a beat. Closing his eyes, he began to sound off the items he would suggest for us to have that evening. Janet listened intently to the verbal menu while I looked for ways to get us the hell out of there in case the "shit" went down. He finished his recital. Janet said everything he had mentioned sounded great and this time, I was the one to nod my approval.

Our main course was going to be a pork loin baked in sorghum, over mashed yams, accompanied by turnip greens and steamed yellow squash. Sweet cornbread and freshly made butter would naturally come with it. Tom suggested to Janet a continuation of the wine she was drinking and for me, Bucklers would add a unique accent to the many flavors we would be enjoying. He bowed to us this time and began to walk away.

Stopping on his third step, he turned back to us and said to me, "The loin is tender, Mr. Madison You won't need your blade to cut it."

Janet looked at me with her "what the hell is he talking about" looks. Having said his piece, Tom continued his retreat to parts unknown, leaving me to face the music.

I slowly brought my hand up from under the table and told Janet the reason for my actions. She listened to me with a look on her face that could break bricks. After I explained about Tom's teeth as well as the ring and all, she slowly calmed to a point that I felt my life would be preserved that night. I apologized to her profusely and made a joke that eased the tension between us.

Our salads arrived soon, brought to us by a young woman. Janet asked her about the restaurant's history. The server told us that the Sbisa had been there since the 1860's and had had many owners. The owners today had acquired it through the death of previous owners, an inheritance of sorts. She told us that it was a multi-floored establishment, three to be exact. The main dining area was on the first level, and the second level was the balcony and "party" area during the Mardi Gras. The third level had been the living area, but now it was used for weddings and formal gatherings; however, it was haunted. When she said haunted, Janet and I burst into laughter. The server looked at us as though we were either pie-eyed drunk or crazy. Janet and I managed to subdue our mirth and apologize to the young woman for our outburst. Janet said that a haunted house wasn't too far off course for us. The young woman said that she was surprised to hear us laugh, considering we knew MR. Stringfellow. That sobered us up. The server walked away leaving us to our first course and our thoughts as to what the eery element surrounding our dinner meant.

After we had finished our salads, Tom appeared with small cups of sherbet to "cleanse" the palate as it were. Janet mentioned that the young lady who brought us our salads told us the history of Sbisa and we would like to see the entire establishment and suggested he be our tour guide about the place.

He looked at us in a concerned manner, then he said, "I will show you everything but the third floor. It is locked and not for public viewing."

I countered with, "She told us it was for wedding parties and formal occasions. She also told us it had been used as the living quarters for previous owners. What's so scary about that?"

Janet looked at Tom with a coquettish air and he

relented from his original doctrine.

"If the lady would like to see the area, I will see to it, but I warn you now, there is a presence there that may or may not be friendly. If the latter, you may be in peril. If Mr. Stringfellow was here tonight, he would protect you I'm sure, but alas, I'm not able to fend off the spirit myself."

I took all this claptrap in stride. I nodded our awareness of danger and made sure my reality tools were at the ready for an intersession of trouble.

Upon insisting he show us, we followed Tom back through the door into the main dining area. He immediately turned left and moved to a staircase. I watched the doors to the rooms in this area and heard muffled conversations. Strong odors of delicious concoctions filled my nose and I almost wanted to stop there for a while and just breathe. Janet tugged my arm and I hesitantly moved my body to follow. Taking the first few steps cleared my head. Tom was talking about the Mardi Gras and the hordes of people that used the second floor for their parties. At that, he took us out onto the balcony to see the milling crowds just a few feet below us. He was right; it was a choice spot to enjoy the revelry.

Back out into the hallway with the stairwell leading to this floor, there was a section of the staircase chained off and padlocked that lead up to the third floor. Janet and I stood there waiting for Tom to pull a key from a pocket and unlock the padlock. Janet said that it was an awfully old padlock. I glanced down at the lock and noticed that it was huge by today's standards and really old. I picked it up in my hand and in doing so, caused the chain to rattle somewhat. Tom stepped back at the sound of the chain being moved and a cold wind surged past me and Janet, making her shiver. It felt like a cool breeze to me and I enjoyed it. Tom's eyes turned white, like he'd been dead for a long time, and all the color drained from his sockets. I thought he was going to faint. I reached out to catch him, grabbing onto his right arm and when I did, he reached out and grabbed mine to steady himself. Unless I was tripping again, the hand that grabbed me wasn't really a hand. For a second it took the shape of a ... a talon, I guess. Hell, things were happening so fast, I could have been caught up in the "freak" of the moment and could have made up all the hoodoo in my head.

I gently let Tom slide down to the floor and looked for Janet. She had disappeared. I thought for a second I would have to drop old Tom and look for her, when I heard her voice along with someone telling someone else to get some water. She appeared around the corner with "suit man" and a couple of regular serving people. I lay Tom's head on down to the floor. One of the servers took some cold water from a pitcher and put it on one of the restaurant's cloth napkins. They, in turn, made a compress and put it on Tom's forehead. Upon the application of the compress, Tom began to flop around like a dying fish. Then, with a shake that permeated his whole body, he just laid there. His eyes sprung open and he rolled over facing the floor. He pushed his arms out forward and placed his fingertips on the floor as though he were hanging on a cliff as he dug into the floor with his fingernails. What surprised me next startled me so abruptly that I didn't believe a human being could do what I saw.

Tom, having his fingers entrenched into the floor, placed the toes of his shoes in the same manner as his fingers and begin inching his way toward his middle like an inchworm. We all watched as his shoes and fingers met. Tom let out a scream of pain that was heard throughout the restaurant. I heard people gasping and the breaking of dishes. Tom's arms were flung out to the sides of his body making him look like a diver coming off the board. He was still up on his toes. His whole demeanor was of a puppet.

He began to inch forward on his toes. His fingers began to wave as if he were trying to take flight. He swung around and faced the stairs to the third floor. His mouth opened exposing his canines and what seemed like rows of sharpened teeth. Great puddles of drool proceeded from his mouth. He began to gnash at the chain. Grunting, slobbering sounds came from deep down in his guts. He stood, floated, flopped, and contorted while his teeth were breaking off on the links of the chain. I had encircled Janet with my arms to keep her from anything that came our way because of the bugga boo crap that was going on.

Janet leaned onto me and whispered for me to let her go. I looked into her eyes and saw that she was okay and I could do as she had asked. I let her go and she immediately moved to Tom. She reached out and touched "drool boy" and he fell to the floor like a lead balloon. His breathing was sharp and full. Janet kneeled down and laid her hand on the back of his head. His breathing calmed and he seemed to fall asleep. Everyone, including myself, stood there dumbfounded. Finally, I blurted out that someone needed to call an ambulance.

I went to Janet as she kneeled next to Tom. She looked up at me and said it was "Grand Mal." Of course she knew because she was on top of things. I looked at her as though she had said something in an alien language while she proceeded to tell me that some people who are subject to epileptic seizures, sometimes have what is known as "Grand Mal" seizures that are more pronounced and more dangerous than normal seizures. Tom had had a bad one.

The sound of the ambulance began to blare as it pulled up to the front door of the restaurant. The EMTs moved through the crowd that had gathered and proceeded to apply their expertise. One of the medics asked, to no one in particular, what had taken place and Janet spoke up reciting the scene and her actions. When she had finished telling the story, the E.M.T. looked at her and asked if she were a doctor or a nurse. Janet explained that her work in the medical field during her early years as a blood technologist taught her that the more a person learned about these sort of situations, the better they could handle emergencies. Time was of the essence in most emergencies and luckily for her, she had worked around medical professionals who weren't anal, as a lot of them are.

The EMTs got Tom onto the gurney and rolled him toward the ambulance. The manager of the restaurant was going to ride with him and take care of the paperwork at the hospital. Before he left, he told "suit boy" to take care of us and give us anything we wanted, cart blanche. I could dig that. Janet and I made it back to the courtyard and were immediately bombarded by "wait" persons wanting to do and bring us everything in the restaurant. We settled for our original dinner and asked to be left alone, but were checked on periodically.

I looked at Janet in the candlelight and the reflected light of the pool. She blushed and told me to quit. I told her she was amazing. I asked her to explain to me how she knew all this stuff and had kept it a secret from me all these years. She said she would tell me later, but as for now, she was still on sabbatical and all she wanted to do was to finish the night in peace and quiet. I nodded agreement and dropped the questions. It was the least I could do for us.

We ate and finished the evening meal with a caramel praline terramasou, then decided to walk leisurely back to the condo. Arm in arm, we headed away from Sbisa. I turned to look back at the restaurant and wondered about the bugga boo spirit and the third floor we never got to see. Janet tugged at my sleeve and said to leave it alone. We looked at the shops along the way and the people who crawl out of the woodwork at the first sign of darkness. The old man yelling through the portable microphone and speaker about God and repentance while standing in front of a strip joint was the kicker for me. I laughed until I cried. What a city.

When we returned to the condo, I made a pot of CDM while Janet changed into lounging clothes. After I got the coffee going, I also slipped out of my "fancy" clothes and into a pair of gym shorts and a Tee shirt. I got Janet a cup of coffee and one for myself as we flopped onto the couch. We both leaned back into the deep pillows. With our eyes closed, I just about fell asleep, coffee or not. Everything got so quiet, the silence was too loud. My sensitive brain woke up and told me something was amiss.

I sat straight up from my laid back position and sure enough, the damn phone rang. Janet jumped. I looked at the phone and didn't even try to pick it up. Janet reached across my lap and picked up the receiver. I watched her face after she said hello. Her face became like stone. She handed the phone out to me and said, "Snid." I took the phone and stared at her with my best F----- you stare and she shrugged her shoulders as she grimaced.

I spoke into the phone only saying, "What!" There was the ever annoying silence for a moment, then the grating voice of Snid.

"It is time to finish this. Start your equipment and prepare."

Silence ensued with the click of the phone being hung up on the other end and the buzz of the dead line. I hung up the receiver. As I turned to Janet, she was picking up her pad and pen.

She looked over at me and said, "So much for fun and relaxation." I couldn't say anything at that.

I got up and walked over to the VCRs and with remotes in hand, hit the magic buttons and sat back down next to Janet. During the initial snow, I told her I was sorry

188

about all this crap. She patted me on my leg.

Ce's head filled the TV screen. He was so close to the camera his eyeball loomed at us as though it were trying to go from Ce's face into the room we were in. We heard noise coming from behind Ce and a quick blur of shadow let us know that Snid was also there. Off in the distance of our reality, Janet and I heard thunder. A storm was brewing on the bayou. Ce's big eye gave way to backing into his chair and as he sat down, I surveyed his room. It still looked as though he lived in a funeral parlor. It didn't take Ce long to get situated. Then, he immediately began his narrative.

Good evening, David and Janet. I have just returned from the hospital. I am happy to tell you that Tom is out of any danger now, even the danger you placed him in." I looked at Janet.

"Yes". Ce said, "the danger you subjected him to at the restaurant. You two are magnets for those elements that seem to wreak havoc on this plane. As it were, Louisiana is somewhat a portal for these entities. Let us finish our business here, and you can go home away from 'opportunities' of this ilk." Ce never skipped a beat and went right back to telling me and Janet about Dad.

Dick drove the wagon and maneuvered it down the alley behind the store. Outside the back door off to the left was a shed where the "boys" kept their supply of sugar. J, By appearance, it seemed to be just a shed. John told Dick that it was the usual routine to pick up the sugar on the backside of the shed that faced the wall of another building. Dick looked at John for a minute and wondered if the boy had any woodsman's skills at all. In the woods it was easy to get into a lot of places, but getting out was another matter. Dick surveyed the area and decided the best thing to do was to go straight down the center of the shed from the back. This would leave the whole alley open for an escape, keeping him and the sugar dry during bad weather. Being inside the shed would also keep prying eyes from seeing him take care of business.

John protested a little when Dick pulled the wagon into the shed instead of stopping at the back of the shed. Dick stared him down and John's protest stopped. After Dick tied off the reins, he jumped off the wagon and immediately went to shut the back door and lock it. Moving to the front of the shed, he stuck his head out the big double doors there and scoped out the alley. To his hunter's eye, the movements of the town folk passing the entrance to the alley meant nothing was different.

Dick closed the big doors and secured them with an old hayfork that was leaning against the front wall. Having moved the wagon inside meant John would have to work harder to get the bags of sugar on the wagon and he mumbled to himself about the weight of each bag when he picked one up. Dick, on the other hand, felt each bag get lighter as he relished the work that made his young muscles pull and tug. He kept a count of the bags and mentally calculated the total in his head for future reference.

When all the bags were loaded, the boys had worked up a sweat. John said that he usually went to the store after loading the wagon and Mr. Greg would give him a cold pop out of the icebox.

Dick looked at John and said, "Not today. We'll get the sugar to its place and then we'll collect our pay. I know where there are a couple of cold springs on the way and we'll get a drink there."

John almost started to whine when Dick's stare

stopped him. Looking into Dick's eyes, John could only mutter a sheepish okay.

Dick bounded onto the wagon and snatched the reins. He told John to open the big doors and get on board. John ran at this task as if his underwear was on fire. He ran mostly because he was mad at Dick for being so strong and of course, he was mad about getting water instead of his usual pop. Dick let the horses meander through the doors and when they started to pull to the right, he let them have their way. John spoke up and told Dick he was going the wrong way. Dick didn't say anything and let the horses plod down the alley.

When they got to the end, Dick turned them north and they traveled along the main drag for a few minutes. Dick then turned the left and circled back to the alley and down to the other end. John asked him what the hell was wrong with him. Dick said that if anyone was watching for them to come out of the alley straight away after they first started, going the other way would make the watcher move to see where they were headed. By the time the watcher maneuvered through the streets the way they were laid out, he and John could circle back and be on their way before the watcher was able to get to the other end of the alley. John just shook his head in disbelief.

On their way to the stills, Dick stopped twice for cold water to give John and the horses. John griped, but the horses were delighted. Dick queried John about why the horses were so happy. John said he never stopped for water before. He let them drink at the barn after he got back from his run. Dick shook his head this time and thought about the treatment of "dumb animals." All the while he kept staring at John. After the horses drank some water, though not so much to have made them sick, Dick and John made their way to the assigned still and unloaded their cargo of sugar. John was still bitching about his pop and how hard this run had been. Usually the "shiners" had to unload the wagon, but Dick thought it would be best if he and John did it in order to keep tabs on the bags of sugar. At the end of the day when he went to get his money, everything would be tit for tat. Dick followed his plan so when the work day came to a close and he accounted for that day's run to Mr. Greg, he was impressed with Dick's commitment to the job and paid him promptly.

Dick got his money and shared it with his mother. She was delighted to be able to send off for a new hat and reminded Dick that she needed more money. Dick was ready with a reply this time. He told her she would get what he gave her and not a cent more. This "hurt" her feelings and she went into a crying jag. Dick finally relented and gave her another fifty cents and miraculously her crying stopped. Dick got to keep two of the five dollars. And to him, he was self-supporting now.

He went back to the store and bought a couple of cans of beans, a magazine, some coal oil for his lamp, an apple, and a pop. Mr. Greg was there talking to Billy and as Dick was leaving, Mr. Greg hollered for Dick to come over and have a word. Dick hesitated at first because of Billy being there, but shrugged it off as just a coincidence. Mr. Greg told Dick that he was going to get to use another wagon and make runs by himself. Seemed Billy didn't want his boy, John, hanging around Dick. Dick shrugged this off, too. He was elated that he would be on his own and able to get things done without "whiny boy" being there.

When Dick smiled at the suggestion he would be his own "man," Billy turned red as a beet. With Billy's reaction, the hair on the back of Dick's neck prickled. Dick knew something was up and he'd have to keep an eye on "old" Billy.

The thunder Janet and I had heard earlier, increased in loudness to the point I noticed the flashes of lightning outside coming through the window. I began thinking to myself, that's all we needed, was a storm to knock out the power and we'd be stuck there longer. Ce never missed a beat. He continued on. The storm increased in its intensity. Janet wrote and I sat on the couch like the proverbial lump. I was so tired of this shit.......

"David!"

I was brought back from the zone I'd fallen in when I heard my name yelled out. I looked around the room at Janet, and back at the "idiot" box. Ce was still talking, but he looked really annoyed. He stopped talking.

He said, "Do you mind? Pay attention. I'm not telling this story again and *you* will show me the courtesy of listening to me, young man."

I felt as though I was about 4 years old and had just been scolded by a babysitter. I looked at Janet and she looked amused and flushed.

I managed to squeak out, "Sorry." Ce grunted his acceptance of my apology. He adjusted his seating arrangement and began his narrative again.

The prickling on the back of your father's neck had been prophetic. As the days went by and Dick made his runs as well as more money, he noticed little things along his routes that began to play on his instincts. It was intuitive notice that Dick took like a shadow in the woods off the path he'd take. Or the noise of breaking branches from the woods around the still when he took a break after unloading his wagon. The kicker was the number of footprints Dick found around one of his stops. Those footprints told of many people being in a place where there were normally only one or two. Dick mentioned his trepidations to Mr. Greg, who frowned when he told him.

"Dick, old hoss, be careful and alert. Sounds like 'John Law' has found our stills. But, for the life of me, I don't understand why they're just watching and not running in with axes to bust the stills up."

Dick told Mr. Greg that he'd be alright and if he saw anything important, he'd let him know as fast as he could. Mr. Greg patted Dick on the head and Dick took off to give money to his mother.

A couple of days later, all hell broke loose. Dick had picked up his "supply" at the store and headed out to make his run. There were just a certain number of ways a person could go in a wagon with a load and not end up mired down axel deep in mud. Dick knew all those roads and tried not to use the same way every day. This day however, it didn't matter. Dick was watching his surroundings as he passed out of the town proper. That feeling he got when he knew something was about to happen eased onto him enough to make him stop dead still. He could tell by the horses pull and tug that something was amiss. Dick strained every fiber he could muster of his skill as a hunter to try and discern what was about to happen, but to no avail.

Two men came out of the woods a few feet from where Dick had stopped. They both had shotguns and when they got to the path Dick was on, they stopped and faced him. Dick's first instinctive thought was to jump and run He'd talked to Mr. Greg about this and Mr. Greg told Dick that escape was okay. A boy Dick's age didn't need to spend time in jail. Dick heard the sound of a pump shotgun being primed from the back of the wagon and he swiveled around to see the cause of that noise. About halfway in his turn, Dick's head exploded. His body went limp and he fell off the seat of the wagon landing face down. He knew he wasn't shot, but his mind was fuzzy enough to make him just lay where he was. But, the pain from the blow cleared the fuzzies out fast. His jaw was busted. He opened an eye and looked at the wagon. Billy was standing on the back holding a pump shotgun.

While Dick was watching the two men in front of him, Billy must have snuck out of the woods and made a beeline to the wagon. Dick was good at hunting animals. Animals had habits and reason behind their movements. Men, it seemed, were more devious. Dick learned a life lesson that day. If you have to fight to get your point across to somebody, kill'em, or they or someone they know will come back to haunt you.

Dick was almost sick with pain. Billy lowered himself off the wagon. He waved to the two men in the path to come on back to the wagon. As they approached, Billy went to where Dick lay.

He leaned down to Dick and shouted, "You bastard, how does it feel now that I'm the one fuck'n you over. You're the one down now, ain't you boy."

With that, Billy kicked Dick in the ribs, hard. It was hard enough to raise Dick off the ground a foot or two. He felt the air rush from his lungs and his side cave in. He tried to get up, but now as well as his jaw, he had busted ribs, too. The other two men came to where Dick was laid out. He got a look at them for just a second. One was the sheriff Dick had crossed and he didn't recognize the other one. Dick faintly heard the sheriff say, "dumb bastard." More pain flushed over him and he passed out.

When Dick awoke, he was mid-air in freefall. His body had been thrown off the old Street Bridge that spans the Harpeth River. He wasn't aware of any of that though, because he thought he was having a dream. That is, until he hit the water. Dick's tattered body slapped the river face down. A million shards of stinging pain seared his entry into the muddy water. The cold shock and his natural instinct to stay alive, threw Dick's mind into high gear. He let his natural buoyancy bring him back up to the surface out of the river's depth. The current was fast enough to keep him moving at a fast clip. So as soon as he felt his nose leave the water, he rolled and sucked as much air in his bruised lungs as he could, then he rolled over again into a dead man's float and held his breath allowing the current the job of getting him away from the would-be killers. It was all he could do to keep from screaming out loud, losing all the precious air that pushed against his swollen lungs.

Within a minute, he was swept around a bend in the river known as the "narrows." Dick didn't realize this or much of anything. Again, he was passing out. Water was sucked into his nostrils and this shook the life into him along with his fear. He threw the yoke of pain away and started to swim. Eventually, he pushed out of the strong current and made it to the bank. The water shallowed out the closer he got to land. By the time he reached shore, he was literally dragging himself across a sandbar. He took an abrogated look around and then his head collapsed to the sand and he lay there until nightfall.

Dick was one of those people that had a natural constitution that, even as a child, afforded him an exaggerated resilience. Even while he lay on the sandbar, his body went into healing, at least enough to keep him from dying on the spot. When he woke up the next time, the sun was barely shining through the tree-lined shore. Nightfall loomed over the river. Dick tried to "jump" up from where he laid. When he exerted his muscles, he let out a howl, coughed, sneezed, and farted, all at the same time and never moved an inch. The opening of all those normally closed body passages at one time, shot a rush of air through his entire interior cavity and organs that had never seen the light of day, saw twilight.

Dick floundered where he lay. All the body juices that lubricate the muscles and joints were excreting after the "cleansing." He moved slower the next time and found that steady movements, not ballistic, were called for. What seemed like hours to him only took a few minutes as Dick found himself sitting up sideways, gradually pushing himself up with his right arm. He drug his feet under himself and pushed up to a kneeling position. Then he stood, sort of. His upper body leaned forward like he was hunching his shoulders. He felt woozy. Trying to steady himself against the night air, he lurched forward and stumbled to the treeline where he caught hold of a trunk and hugged it for dear life. He sucked the cooling night air into his lungs in sharp gulps. It was painful, but he knew if he tried to breathe too deeply, he'd pass out from the pain the expansion of his rib cage would cause. It was a long night that he was not likely to ever forget.

Struggling from tree to tree and not knowing exactly where he was, for the first time ever, Dick was afraid of the woods. He was so busted up, he couldn't focus. He pushed on though out of anger, out of pain, out of the thoughts for revenge. He fell from time to time, pulling himself up by grasping vines and small limbs. He moved on. His body cried out for him to stop, fall down, die; it was tired. Before he would let weakness overcome him, he would take a deep breath or move his jaw so the pain sharpened his will to move on. Before dawn, he stopped. Bent over and gasping for air, he heard a familiar sound of a dog barking so he knew he was close to someone's house and if he could see it, he'd know where he was. Then, he'd get to his momma. His feet felt as if he were trying to drag lead weights through the weeds and brush that surrounded him. The dog's bark got louder as he moved forward. Finally he broke through the woods and stood at the edge of a field. He could see the main house from the spot he was standing. He recognized it. It was Red's house.

He said out loud, "Thank God." A new strength filled his broken body and he kept moving as if he were drunk, but he moved. Finally he got to the back of his momma's house. He saw his father leave for the mill. Dick counted the seconds, minutes. After he told himself that his father was gone for real, he moved to the house. He almost fell up the back stairs that lead to the porch and the kitchen door. He got to the door and managed to let out a weak, "Momma." Bessie must have been near the door to have heard him. She swung the door open and seeing Dick, her eyes widened at the appearance of her son. She and Dick stood there for a minute staring without any words passing between them. Dick couldn't hold himself up any longer. He slid to the kitchen floor, spread eagle at his momma's feet. She got out an "Oh my God, Dick."

Bessie looked out the back door to see if anyone was lurking around. When she had satisfied herself that Dick was alone, she slammed the door and turned her attention to him. His face had turned blackish blue and his jaw was distorted to one side. She saw down into his overalls that he was bruising there, too. She told him to lay still and she would be right back. Dick tried to grab her arm to keep her from leaving him. As he raised his right arm, pain shot through him like shit through a goose and it was strong enough to make him pass out.

His next recollection was when he felt the wire being pulled through his jaw. He was being wired shut. He woke sporadically. Once he woke and he knew he was in a bed, but he didn't know where. The few times someone was near when he woke, they were strangers. During his "outs", Dick dreamed; he dreamed of woods and deer, fish, and Bad Eye. He dreamed of being in the "hole."

Eventually Dick woke and didn't fall right out again. It took him a while to focus. When he got his bearings, he tried to sit up, but the busted ribs and the other damage to his internals let him know he was going to be on his back for awhile. He tried to ask for some water and that was when he realized that his mouth was shut tight. A few minutes went by.

A nurse making her rounds stopped by his bed and saw he was awake. She smoothly patted his head and went for the doctor. Dick grunted as loud as his body would let him. The nurse stopped halfway to the door and came back to the bed. Dick grunted again. He moved his eyes toward the pitcher on the little table by his bed. The nurse caught on to his signal and poured him some water. She opened the drawer of the table and pulled out a straw. Putting it into the water, she worked the straw between Dick's lips and he sucked the cool liquid into his mouth and swallowed. He drank that glass of water. He wanted more, but the nurse said it wasn't good to get too much in his condition. She put the glass next to the bed. She left the room this time.

A few minutes later, a man came in and picked up a chart at the end of the bed and looked at Dick with an air of gentry and peasant. The doctor said nothing to Dick, but addressed everything to the nurse. Dick wanted to know how bad of shape he was in, but it would be another two weeks before he could mumble through his clenched mouth. The doctor asked Dick if he could write and Dick begrudgingly nodded, yes. The doctor handed Dick a pad and pencil and told Dick to make his requests or ask any questions by writing them down.

Dick hurriedly wrote on the pad, "How did I get here?" The doctor told him his mother had brought to the hospital in a wagon. "Where's here?" Dick scribbled.

"You're at Vanderbilt Hospital, son. In Nashville."

"Where's my mother?" Dick wrote.

"She said she had to get back home and that she would drop in on you as soon as she could. Well, I've got rounds tonight, nurse. Keep an eye out for our boy here; this new procedure of wiring a broken jaw is just that, new." The nurse thanked the doctor who patted Dick on his head, then left the curtained room and went to the next patient.

Dick hurriedly wrote on the tablet, "How long am I going to be trussed up like this, M'am?" He made a noise and the nurse took the pad from him. She read the question and replied by telling Dick that he'd be in the hospital for approximately 6 to 8 weeks. With the broken ribs, the bruised spleen, and the broken jaw, it would take awhile for him to recuperate. Dick's heart sank to the depths of dark depression at that point. He took the pad from the nurse. When she asked him if he needed anything else, he shook his aching head, no. She also patted him on the head as she left the area, pulling the curtain closed behind her.

Dick lay there helpless and alone. The minutes seemed to pass by like years and finally sleep managed to take hold of him again. He spent the next few days hoping to see his mother. She did not come. After the third week without visitors, Dick steeled his resolve and said to hell with it. He was just able to walk a bit during his fourth week in the hospital when he advantageously positioned himself near the nurses' station where he couldn't be seen, but he could hear anything and everything the nurses talked about giving him a chance to find out when he would leave.

On that day, Dick heard that his mother couldn't get the money to keep Dick in the ward at the hospital anymore. If someone didn't come get him soon, he'd be sent to the reform school and recuperate in their clinic. Dick thought to himself, I am not going to any reform school, and I haven't done anything wrong. As he planned his escape, he knew he wasn't in any shape to go too far, but he would rather die than be in a prison.

Dick planned all through the night. He planned so

hard when he was awakened by his mother's voice, he thought he was dreaming. He opened his eyes to see his mother standing with a man. He sort of looked familiar to Dick, but he couldn't place him. Bessie explained to Dick that the man was his cousin, Johnny Potts. He was from Chicago. As soon as Dick heard the name, Potts, he knew who this man was. He was a cousin on his momma's side of the family, the side that went up north when their family farm went sour. That was up north to the land of Yankees and work. Cousin Johnny looked dapper if you will. He sported a white hat along with a shirt and tie. He had real pants on and shoes, not farm boots, but real shined shoes. Johnny smiled.

"Dick, you're going to come home with me, up to Chi town. Arrangements have been made for you to stay with me and my mother, your Aunt Edith. My boss, Mr. Capone, has a doctor friend that will look in on you from time to time and when you're healed enough, take the wire out of your jaw."

If he could have yelled out loud, he would have screamed bloody murder. He wrote frantically on the pad and almost threw it at his mother. She read what he'd written without even blinking an eye. When she finished reading, she looked at Dick and shook her head.

"Son", she said, "we can't afford this place anymore. I've borrowed from your grandfather and he won't lend me any more money. After what you did to your father, he wouldn't spit on you if you were on fire. I didn't know what else to do so I got in touch with your Aunt Edith. She sent Johnny down here to get you."

At that, she leaned over Dick and kissed him on the forehead. She then turned, touched Johnny on the arm, and walked away from the bed.

Dick, lay there for a second, and then tried to get himself up to go to her. She never stopped to look back, but just kept walking. Dick dropped down to the bed again and stared at his cousin.

Johnny fidgeted for a few minutes, then a nurse came in and told Johnny to wait out in the hall while she helped Dick to dress. Dick hurt and he realized that he was in no shape to put up a fight. The nurse helped him stand up. Dick almost fell from the rush he got from getting up. The nurse was ready though and caught him. She untied his gown and marveled at how well developed he was from the waist down. She smiled at him and he blushed the darkest shade of red. The nurse helped him on with his overalls. Someone had washed them. Dick's nose had regained most of its sense of smell. The nurse spoke in a loud voice asking Johnny to come back in the area. Johnny saw Dick and said he'd been told Dick was a good-sized boy.

Dick stood by himself for a minute while Johnny spoke to the nurse about Dick's food and such. She gave him a list of soft foods he could get Dick. He began to lose his balance, then he felt the strong hands of Johnny Potts reach out and grab his arm. Dick managed to put an arm on Johnny's shoulder and the two began to walk away from the ward. The nurse followed, and as they passed the nurses' station, she stopped and told Dick goodbye. He would have grinned, but all he could do was nod his head.

Johnny got Dick to the parking area and walked him to his truck. He leaned Dick on the side of the truck and opened the passenger door. Dick had been in the sheriff's truck, now in his cousin's truck. Johnny helped Dick get in, then ran to the driver's side and got in. He looked at Dick. "Boy you ought to be thankful those old boys didn't kill you. Anyway, that's past now. You'll like it up in Chi town. It's hot in the summer and damn cold in the winter."

Dick liked it where he was from in the Tennessee country. Chicago could and would be a whole new world for him. A big, man filled, stinking city. Dick looked out of

the truck's window as Johnny headed north toward
Chicago. Dick saw the woods and rivers he loved pass by
him at the speed of thirty miles an hour. He thought of his
momma a minute, then he shrugged it off. Johnny had been
talking a blue streak all the while, but Dick paid him no
mind. Dick leaned back in the seat as far as he could and let
the drone of Johnny's voice lull him to sleep.

Ce threw his head forward and looked straight
ahead into the camera. When he spoke this time it was as if
he were in the room with Janet and David.

"Listen you two, I'm exhausted. Could we forgo
the rest of your father's story for now? I really need to rest
and I dare say, you two need to be getting back to
Memphis."

Janet and I sat there looking at one another for a
moment with disbelief, thankful this whole thing was at an
end, but disappointed we did not know the whole story. I
sat there and dumbly nodded yes to Ce's question.

"Good, good," said Ce. "Please leave the tapes in
the hall and I'll have Snid pick them up. Your friend
Hobart will be by soon and will give you the 'all's clear'
for you to leave town. I believe he's found the culprit who
committed the eradication of those evil men. Well now, I
must bid you adieu, for the present." The screen went to
snow.

I jumped off the couch and hit the STOP buttons
instead of using the remotes. I looked at Janet and asked
her if she was ready to get the hell out of there, I hope?
Janet spoke up and returned my quip with a sarcastic, if
you're waiting on me, you're behind the times, 'cause I've
already left. She sprang up and headed toward the
bedroom, pads and pen in hand. I gathered up the tapes
from Ce and put my copies in a pile on the coffee table.

Ce's copies went into a paper sack. I walked to the

door and as I was about to open it, I heard a faint staccato knock. It was as Ce said, Hobart. I stood there with my bag of tapes and looked at him with a, "well?" look. He pushed past me into the condo. I laid the tapes out in the hall and closed the door behind him. Without as much as a "kiss my ass," he started talking.

"I've got to admit, you people are the weirdest I've come across in a long time, and I've come across a bunch. I'm here to tell you that you can go, and I suggest that you go as fast as the law allows."

I interrupted him at this point and said, "So, you're telling me that we're no longer suspects in this case."

"Yes, we apprehended a man from out in the boondocks that was bragging about the two dead guys being a tasty treat." He told us he'd stolen things from a cab driver and a lot of crap about zombies and a maniac with a thousand knifes.

"Anyway, you're free to go and stay gone, if you get my meaning."

I opened the door and pointed to the hall. Hobart moved out to the hall and neither he nor I said anything. I looked to make sure the tapes were where I'd left them, yeah, right. They were gone. I closed the door and hurried to the bedroom.

Janet was wrestling with the suitcase so I grabbed it. Everything was packed. The damn thing weighed a ton. I slipped on the shoes she'd left out for me. We made sure to grab our V.C.R. and made sure no electrical stuff was left on. Janet scribbled a note to the condo manager and we headed to our car. Ten minutes later, we were gone.

Prologue

Janet slept most of the way back to Memphis. I was so wired, all I could do to keep from jumping out of my seat was to make sure I was buckled up. I thought about the past few days, mainly about my dad and Ce. I grew a little melancholy. I missed him.

We got home with no problem. Our son, Robert, had been home and had gotten the mail for us. I put the suitcases in the bedroom and was going back to the car to get the V.C.R. and our other things, when I heard Janet laugh and say. "Oh, my God!" I stopped heading for the car and went to see what was up. She was holding a letter and what looked like tickets. She turned, when I came up to her and handed me the letter which read, *You have won the New Orleans raffle to Rome, Italy for two. Two weeks, all expenses paid.* Blah, blah, blah.

Tickets were enclosed with vouchers for a hotel. *Enjoy your stay and thank you for helping our children.* I looked at Janet and I burst out laughing. She handed me another envelope. It was addressed to me in a script reminiscent of an old hand cursive like one would see on copies of the "Bill of Rights and the Constitution." There was no return address. I opened it. It began,

"David, I am glad you have won the trip to Rome. She is quite the city. Your father was there during the war, you know. I look forward to seeing you and your lovely wife there so I can tell you the story of how your father and I came to know each other. Until then,
Ceophulus T. Stringfellow

I handed the letter to Janet. She read it out loud. When she came to the part about "until then", we began to laugh. I hugged her, she squeezed me, and then, we kept laughing.

Meet the Author

**Dave Putnam has written a story about
real people entwined in truth and legend,
drawing from his father's life and his own.
Dave was born in Nashville, Tennessee.**

One Bone Rattle

For Additional Copies

Send $12.95 (per copy)
+ 3.95 Shipping

Check or Money Order to:

IAMPress
**3053 Dumbarton Road
Memphis, TN 38128
901.358.2226
E-mail: iampress@iam-cor.org**

Please Allow 2-3 Weeks Delivery